COWBOY

COWBOY

FRANK RODERUS

DOUBLEDAY & COMPANY, INC.
GARDEN CITY, NEW YORK
1981

All of the characters in this book are fictitious,
and any resemblance to actual persons, living or dead,
is purely coincidental.

Library of Congress Cataloging in Publication Data

Roderus, Frank.
Cowboy.

I. Title.
PS3568.0'346C6   813'.54
ISBN: 0-385-17120-X
Library of Congress Catalog Card Number 80-1866
First Edition

For Jean and Dave Naquin

COWBOY

CHAPTER 1

I grew up in this business and I like it, and that's why I've stayed in it. I don't at all mind being called Cowboy, although nowadays there seem to be a good many fellows who object to it as a word much less as a name. I don't know why. It's been in use since back in the '50s.

Come to think of it, there were cowboys back during the American Revolution. If I remember my history correctly, back then they were Tories, a bunch of colonists loyal to the King, who had a sort of guerrilla warfare going with us Rebel types. Probably stole cows from the good guys. Anyway, I think we've lived down that meaning of the word since the Revolution. After all, that was quite a few years ago, and we have gone through a few other pretty good wars in the meantime, including the Great War just ended.

The boys who went off to that one are back now, the ones that still could come back, and really most of the fellows I knew and used to ride with did come back healthy and excited and full of tall tales about Fritz and—more stories if not much more believable—about Fifi. These days, in fact, you are about as likely to hear a cowboy singing "Mad'moiselle from Armentières" on night herd as you are to hear one of the old traditionals.

A lot of the boys who came back, though, aren't in the business anymore. They went Over There and saw the big cities, got used to sit-down outhouses and sit-down meals and decided when they got home to keep on sitting down on something that wasn't likely to go into a storm and throw them off again.

One nice thing about them being back is that people in town—

the girls in particular, you might say—no longer look at me with the question in their eyes: Why aren't you Over There too?

I did go to sign up, actually. I'm not some damn coffee cooler and would gladly have gone, but back when I was a kid one time I got into a wreck on a bad horse and he mashed up my arm some, the left one it was, so that I can't quite straighten it anymore. It doesn't keep me from doing a darn thing including shooting a rifle, but it kept the Army from passing me. I still don't understand that, but I sure couldn't walk around trying to tell passing strangers about it. I am glad that time is over.

One of the bad things about them being home is that now the price of beef has been going down again. During the war beef and just about any other kind of food went kiting up in price to the point where ranchers could afford to pay a man a living wage. Now I am afraid the payroll will be going back down to where it used to be. It hasn't yet, but I have been expecting it to.

Of course, in the long run that might work to my advantage. If beef gets low enough, there are bound to be a good many stockmen who had forgotten to stay husbandmen when things were flush, people who'd made commitments on fancy blooded stock and new houses and Ford automobiles. Some of those fellows might go bust, and if they did it just might be possible for me to pick up a piece of land of my very own.

Having my own place has been my dream for about as long as I can remember. Ever since we lost our place anyway, and that was when I was fifteen, a dozen years ago.

We used to be land owners ourselves, us Russels. Or should it be we Russels? I can't remember now though my parents both were absolute bearcats on the subject of education. They always said just because we were rural was no excuse for us to be rubes. Neither of them could abide any form of laziness, either mental or physical. My grammar has declined since I left home, I guess, but at least I'm not totally ignorant, thanks to them.

The home place that we used to have was down in Texas, in the Panhandle not far from Yellow House Creek where Pop took up grazing rights not long after it was discovered that a windmill would bring up water there nearly anywhere you cared to drill.

We did all right there for quite a while, but Mama died when I was twelve and that seemed to start a chain of things going wrong, just at the time when Pop didn't have the heart to fight things out all the way to the end of his grit. Mostly, they were things that one at a time would have been small. There were Mama's doctor bills. The casing in one of our wells collapsed. Hoof and mouth disease got into what should have been our herd of market steers so that Pop had to borrow to keep us going another year. Things like that one on top of another.

An Amarillo banker took possession of the place in the fall of 1907, with no hard feelings on either side. It was just something that had to be done.

Even so we stayed together as a family, Pop and Terrell and I, working together for people who used to be our neighbors until the spring of '09 when Pop caught pneumonia and just didn't fight that very hard either. He died, but he had waited until all of the old debts had been paid off, so I like to think he figured it was all right then.

Once he was gone I was ready to quit that country. Terrell wasn't. He is two years older than I and was pretty heavily involved in sparking a yellow-haired girl who lived a couple hours' ride from where we were working at the time.

Terrell decided to stay and I decided to go, and that was that. We wrote back and forth for a while. He never mentioned his girl in the letters, and I don't know if they married or not. After a couple years the letters got farther between, and the last one I wrote was returned with a rubber stamp on it saying the addressee was unknown. Of course, I myself have moved on an average of probably twice a year since I left that country, so it could well be that Terrell has had some letters returned too.

Anyway it's always been my dream to have a place of my own, and for years I've made it a point to put a part of every pay day into an account I keep at a Denver bank. The past few years it had been growing pretty nicely too. Before the war, wages were generally forty a month and keep. Nowadays I was drawing sixty-five dollars and putting aside fifteen of it or sometimes more, depending on how near to a town I was working.

I suppose I could have a lot more money in the bank than I do if I hadn't liked so much to go to town on the weekends, but I enjoy it and that is a fact.

It is *not* a fact, though, that cowboys are mean or nasty or wild in their ways. Town people often seem to think so, but I believe the only difference between us and them is that they spread their relaxation out all through the week while we have to do it all kind of at one time. That's what I tell people, anyhow.

It was on one of those trips into town that things started changing for me. It was a Saturday night so we could take until past the next daylight getting back out to the ranch. I came in with Pete Souchuk and Bertram Taylor.

Pete is one of the new breed of cowboy who travels far between his jobs. He has worked cows in Arizona and in Montana and a good many places in between. He doesn't even own a horse of his own but has a pickup truck that he carries his gear in. He says he can cover as much as two hundred miles in a single day's time that way and reach about any ranch in the country.

Bert goes at things more like I do and keeps his own horse ready for the day he'll decide to move. Still, neither of us is so set in his ways that we don't know a good thing when we see it, so we all piled into Pete's truck for the ride to town. The truck could do in an hour or less what it would take us three hours to ride horseback.

We bounced and clattered our way onto Main Street by 8:30 P.M. and were in a pretty good humor from getting such an early start.

The first thing we had to do, of course, was check out the cinema parlor. I hadn't ever paid all that much attention to moving pictures before, but a few weeks ago the name of one had caught our attention. It was called "The Ropin' Fool," and they had a trick roper in that show who was doing things that until then I would have sworn couldn't be done. We surely enjoyed that picture and would have watched it twice again, but this time they were playing something with an artsy sounding name so Pete drove on by and parked down by the Thirsty Burro saloon, about which a good many jokes have been made but which at least welcomed cowhands for customers. Not every place did that.

"You comin' inside, Cowboy?" Pete asked when we got out to straighten our legs and hobble around for a moment on solid ground again after the beating we'd been taking.

"Naw, I don't reckon."

Bert grinned. "I'm still waiting for the day I see you drunked up, Cowboy."

"That's fine. Keep waiting. Maybe you'll see it sometime."

"Yeah, well, we'll meet you over to Rose's later."

"I'll be by there directly," I told them. Probably I'd get there before them and in better shape to know what I was doing to boot. "I'll see you boys later."

Bert grinned even bigger, and Pete let out a shrill little yip to let everyone know he was coming and tugged his hat down closer to his ears. With them starting out like that I might not see them again until morning.

I watched them into the doorway and wandered on down the street to make a few purchases before the stores closed. I was nearly out of Bugler tobacco and the other boys smoked Durham, which I always hate to bum because of the fine cut. I wanted to get some ice cream too, to which I am addicted, and I could satisfy both needs at the drugstore so I headed that way.

I nodded to the bald-headed fellow who ran the place and took a stool at the marble-top soda counter. This being a busy night the proprietor had help to handle the counter trade, a thin little girl with a poor complexion and eyeglasses but with a bright and cheerful smile of welcome, and another full of eagerness to please when I ordered my triple-dip dish with nuts and chocolate sprinkles. I hadn't seen this one before and hoped the old man would keep her longer than he'd kept the others since I had been here. She seemed nice.

She went off to fill my order, and I swiveled the stool around so I could watch the other shoppers. There were a good many of them inching sideways past each other in the narrow aisles, most of them women and most of the women trying to ride herd on big-eyed children who looked like they were trying to stay on their best behavior but were too excited for their instructions to take very well.

The soda counter stools were only about half full, all the sit-down customers grownups except one boy who seemed more interested in the little girl behind the counter than in the melting dish of ice cream in front of him.

The girl brought my dish and I swung back around and dug into it.

Some fellow wearing a dust-free Stetson and a business suit came and sat beside me. He nodded politely enough my way and ordered himself a cola drink, which he got and finished before I was halfway done enjoying my ice cream. When the man left he left behind him a folded-up newspaper that he had laid on the counter between us. I didn't notice it there until he was gone, so I folded it another lap and put it into my back pocket in case I should see the gentleman again.

I wasn't attaching much importance to a few cents' worth of left-behind newspaper, so I got my Bugler and paid my bill and headed back up the street toward the part of town that didn't have street lights but that did have Rose's place.

CHAPTER 2

We had the morning off but I woke up at five out of habit. I pulled my clothes on and rubbed the sleep out of my eyes and went downstairs. Bert was already there, helping himself to some of the doughnuts and coffee Rose always set out on Sunday mornings.

I gave him a friendly greeting and he scowled at me, so I had some coffee and a couple doughnuts myself while he decided if he was going to rejoin the living.

"Mornin', Cowboy," he said after a little while.

"Glad to see you're so cheerful this morning," I told him. "Is Pete still sleeping?"

Bert rubbed his face some and gave me a gap-toothed grin. "If I remember right, he never made it this far las' night."

"That stuff will kill you someday."

The grin got bigger. "Naw, this was *good* stuff. Brought down from Canada it was. The real McCoy."

"If you believe that, Bert, I've got a flivver I'd like to sell you."

"Yeah, well, it wasn't bad really."

Which probably meant it wasn't as bad as last week's batch had been. Ever since Prohibition stopped the sale of legal whiskey you didn't know what you were getting, and some of it could get pretty nasty. That was one of the reasons I'd quit drinking. The other . . . well . . . there's no need to get into that. You might just say that I don't like myself a whole lot after I've been drinking, and let it go at that.

Not that the new laws had done much, certainly not that I could see, to dry anything up. Maybe it was different back East, but if the law took any effect, it wasn't anyplace that I could tell the difference. The quality of what you could buy was pretty lousy now, but the quantity hadn't changed the least bit.

Anyway, Bert and I finished our makeshift breakfast and said our good-byes to the fellows who were beginning to stir around. None of the girls was likely to be getting up for quite a while yet, so we found our coats and hats and let ourselves out.

The truck wasn't out front. Bert scratched himself and seemed to be doing some pondering. Finally, he brightened and spat and pointed.

"Down there," he said.

We walked half a block and turned up an alley. Sure enough, the truck was parked in there although why they'd have stopped in there I wouldn't pretend to know. Pete was sleeping—passed out I guess would be more accurate—in the truck bed.

"Why don't you drive us home, Cowboy?" Bert asked.

"Why doesn't Pete? It's his truck."

"He'd throw up for sure. That's why I put him back there last night. Prob'ly still stinks anyway."

"I don't know how to drive one of these things."

"I do," Bert said. He went about getting the controls set. Since that question seemed to be decided, I got into the cab and settled down against the door as comfortable as I could hope to get.

Bert managed to get her running and out of the alley so I decided he really did know what he was doing. I pulled my hat down over my eyes and tried to pretend I didn't feel like two pair of dice in a tin cup.

"Wake up, Cowboy!"

"Huh?" He was shaking me by the arm.

"I swear, boy, I don't see how anybody can sleep in one of these contraptions. I wouldn't't've believed it."

"I wouldn't either." But I guess I had. I had that low-down, loggy feeling the way a body will when he goes to sleep when he should be working. "What's up?"

I took a look around me and sure enough we were in the ruts leading from the graded clay highway up to the headquarters of the YL, which was the place where we were working at the time.

I twisted around and took a peak through the glass window to the rear. Pete was still out, rolling a bit from side to side with the motion of the truck but not doing much of anything on his own. He wasn't stiff so I decided he was still alive anyway.

"He's all right," Bert said. "I checked 'im a while ago."

We chugged across the last rise and down to the tangle of buildings and assorted trash that we were calling home. There wasn't any woman here, which always seemed to make a difference in the way a place is kept. I'd told myself I don't know how many times that if I got a place of my own ever, I'd keep it up properly with or without a woman to tend the house. So far there didn't seem to be much prospect of there being a woman. Or a ranch, for that matter.

Bert stopped the truck under one of the half-dozen trees that might have been the reason for locating the headquarters here. Pete still hadn't moved. We got out of the thing and left Pete to come around in his own good time. We didn't have to get any work done today anyhow, so it didn't matter.

By then it was coming onto midmorning, and a couple doughnuts don't make much of a breakfast.

"Think you can hold down some food now?" I asked Bert.

"Either we head for the cook shack or I start chewing on one of Pete's tires, I don't much care which."

"The taste'd be about the same," I agreed seriously.

"No point making Pete mad, I s'pose."

We headed for the cook shed where old Wooly worked and slept and rarely set foot outside. Even if it was Sunday morning, though, we both of us knew better than to expect a hot meal at this time of day. Wooly would've been up in time to put breakfast on the table by 5:15. If we weren't around to eat it, that was our fault, not his.

Sure enough, everything was still on the table, stony cold but right there waiting for us. Cold eggs and a mess of bacon bedded in congealed grease didn't much appeal to me, but beef is about as good cold as it is hot so I sliced off some bread and built myself a couple sandwiches. Bert dug deep into the bacon and eggs, though how he did it on a hungover stomach I don't understand.

There was a dirtied plate on the table, which meant that the boss was over at the house. Wooly wasn't in sight, but then he rarely was, spending most of his time in the little lean-to room off the kitchen. With Bert and Pete and me, that was the whole crew. Maybe it wasn't much of an outfit, but I'd worked for worse. And for some a lot smaller.

Somewhere there was somebody else connected with the YL, but I didn't know who or where he was. The boss of the place wasn't the actual owner but more of a foreman and general manager. I suppose he kept in touch with the owner, but he never said anything about it to the rest of us, and generally speaking, he was pretty easy to get along with. In fact, he got onto us somewhat less than I thought we deserved at times, so that I didn't think he cared all that much about the owner's profits. I guess what I'm saying is I didn't mind working for the guy, but I wouldn't have hired him if I'd been in the owner's place.

After breakfast Bert and I wandered back to the bunkhouse. I was kind of looking forward to a game of checkers, but Bert said he had some leathers to replace on his gear. He changed to an older hat and went off toward the tack shed.

I only had one hat to keep track of myself, so I hung it on a peg, put my Bugler on the shelf and got down my everyday clothes. When I pulled off my good pants I discovered the newspaper I'd found the night before. I hadn't anything else to do so I stretched out on my bunk and unfolded the paper.

It was called the *Ranchland News,* and it was pretty obvious it tried to deliver what the title promised. There were small items of interest from the towns all over eastern Colorado and some parts of western Kansas. I started with the first one and read them right on through, here and there running into a name I knew or mention of a place I'd worked before. The items weren't stiff and stuffy the way some papers are. Instead they were loose and chatty. I liked that.

Toward the back they had a section for advertisements, and I read those too. They were offering bulls and sheep and machinery, hay stackers and harnesses and tractors—both gasoline and steam driven. Stuff like that. I read every one of those too.

The last page had a few more news items, ones that sounded like they were picked up from other papers and reprinted. Those weren't so chatty.

I got halfway through that page before one little item grabbed hold of me and set me up off that bunk and loping toward the boss's place.

"Terry! Terry! Where the hell are you, son?" I busted through the doorway and into the front room, which was the only room of the place that he used. The rest of the rooms in the house had some junk stored in them but weren't really used for anything. The boss was stretched out on his bed taking a nap. "Wake yourself up, Terry. I got to tell you something."

He came up in a hurry, one hand going for his boots and the other for his hat. "What's up?"

"No emergency. I quit." I turned and started back to the bunkhouse. Terry didn't call anything after me, so I guessed it was all right by him.

It didn't take three minutes for me to throw my razor and tobacco and soap into my war bag and roll my good clothes into my bedroll. I grabbed them up, remembered my spurs in time to add them to my collection and headed back out again.

My horse, a decent old bay gelding that was getting a little long in the tooth now but still sound, was in a fenced pasture just south of the corrals. He absolutely couldn't be caught by a man afoot, but he'd always been a sucker for a feed bucket. I banged on a tin bucket a few times and tolled him and a dozen others to me in no time at all. I let the bay lip the oats in the bucket a couple times—if I didn't let him have some he was bound to figure out the trick eventually—and slipped the bridle on. Another couple minutes and I had him saddled and my gear tied on.

"What's all the racket?" Bert asked as I was finishing. "Hell, Cowboy, it looks like you're going somewhere."

"Mostly because I am, I'd bet."

"Where to?"

"Travelin', Bert. Want to come along?"

"It seems awful sudden."

"Uh-huh."

"Which way you headed?"

"West." I swung up into my beat-up Frazier. "Are you coming?"

Bert fingered his chin and scratched at his crotch and thought it over. "It isn't bad here."

"I can't argue that, but there might be a better deal elsewhere, Bert. Come along if you've a mind to."

He had made up his mind now. He shook his head. "Luck to you, Cowboy."

"Luck to you too, cowboy. Maybe I'll run into you again somewhere."

"Likely." He grinned and stuck his hand out and that was that. I turned the bay horse west and sloped out of there.

CHAPTER 3

Now I have heard and I have read a good many stories about this horse traveling a hundred seventy-five miles in a day's time or that one making two hundred and never breaking a sweat. To hear some boys tell it, their horses must sprout wings and fly, and they never have to pause to eat or drink or sleep either. Don't you believe that bull.

Oh, I'm not saying it can't be done. If you have the right horse with the right training and conditioning behind him and the right feeds to fuel him, a good animal can do some remarkable things.

The point is that those things are truly remarkable.

As a matter of down-to-earth practicality, your average horse just can't make marathon rides day in and day out. It would ruin them if it was asked of them. So when you are piling one day's work onto another, without long periods of rest in between, fifty miles a day is about all you should expect, and less would be better.

Anyway, Pete's truck might've made it across the flat grass to the mountains in a day or so, but I sure couldn't. So I had plenty of time to reread and rethink about that little item in the *Ranchland News*.

I tore the article out and tucked it into my billfold for safe keeping, and I guess I read it three or four times a day until I pretty well knew it by heart.

The item was about a business boom for boarding facilities in and near the town of Monument where it was rumored that the mighty XXX ranch was about to go into liquidation. Speculators were of the opinion that the holdings of the ranch could be acquired at twenty cents on the dollar.

Now if that was true the money I had in the bank would go five times as far as normal, and I might well be able to buy my grass now instead of ten or twenty years into the future.

It was a thing to dream and to hope about, and I knew I couldn't pass up the opportunity no matter how slight it might be. I had to try at the very least.

I had, of course, heard of the XXX. It was one of the old ones, and though I'd never worked in that part of the country I had heard of the ranch. Most people, because of the way whiskey bottles are drawn in newspaper cartoons and such, called the XXX the Whiskey Brand and were more likely to recognize that name than the Three-X.

I'm sure I must have heard the name of the man who founded the Whiskey, but I could not recall it if I had. From the size of the place, though, and more from the easy-striking lines of a big brand that could be made with any handy iron—all those easy ones had been taken up early—it was obvious that the Whiskey had to be really old for this part of the country. If I'd been guessing, I would have put it at fifty years or more just on the basis of that brand made with nothing but straight lines.

Doing a little more guessing I decided that maybe the owner of the place had died recently to cause an estate liquidation. Although, come to think of it, a newspaper article surely would have mentioned that. The death of the owner of a ranch that big and that well established would surely be bigger news than his estate sale.

I had three days to think about that and other possibilities, riding all of that third day with the Front Range mountains in sight, before I crossed the railroad tracks and got my last directions from some people at a town called Black Forest.

This was fine country I was in now. The land was rolling but not chippy or real rough. There were some coulees and cuts, enough to give livestock shelter but not so many as to be a bad hazard when they drifted in front of blowing snow.

There were some rounded mesas with scrub oak and other sass on their sides, but mostly the ground was heavily grassed with not much in the way of yucca or cactus to rob the moisture. And judging from the number of trees established on the ridge lines, where the ground would catch wind-dropped snow, there was a good bit of moisture to be had here.

To the west, running north and south as far as the eye could see, there was a wall of mountains rising several thousand feet above the grassland plains. I knew from past rail trips that the Front Range ran a lot farther than my eyes would ever reach.

The mountains were dark with trees and rock, but somehow were very pretty in spite of being worthless for grazing. I suspected that they would also provide shelter from winter storms moving out of the west. South of where I was and jutting well above the rest of the Front Range I could see Pikes Peak, white and rugged in the spring sunshine though the snow was gone from the rest of the mountains. It's a big one, that peak, and I'd been able to see it long before I could see the others.

I was told to follow the railroad north to Monument, so I angled back a little north of the way I'd come in until I picked up the line of the roadbed again.

The man who gave me those directions was just as nice as he could be, but he must have been a native. Me, I was a fool flatlander who hadn't spent any time here before. And if when I took the train through here before someone had told me that there were *two* railroads running along the Front Range, I sure hadn't paid any attention to the information.

What I did was to set out following the wrong railroad. There was another one between me and the mountains, but I didn't know that. When the fellow said railroad I naturally turned around and went back to the rails I knew about.

I rode and rode along those rails and before too many miles was out of sight of any houses, and soon even seemed to be away from fence lines. I did see a couple southbound trains to wave at. The engineers steam-whistled back at me. The fellow back in Black Forest hadn't said how far it was, so I didn't get concerned. When night came and I couldn't see any house lights I just found a likely looking spot, stripped my gear off the bay and lay down where I was. I didn't have any food with me, but I didn't think I was going to starve overnight either.

Nor did I. In the morning I continued on along the railroad tracks for another couple hours before I began to get suspicious that I wasn't going where I wanted to be.

Out in the middle of that open grass I found a railroad siding complete with holding pens and a loading chute and a low dock of the sort that freight can be loaded into or out of rail cars. There wasn't any sign to say whose or where this was.

They had drilled a well, though, and built the holding pens around it. The mill was turned off.

I took the horse on into the pens and found the water tank empty. It wasn't rigged with a float to turn itself on or off, and the pull chain to the trip mechanism was busted. I had to climb the mill tower to turn it on and then wait there while the steady breeze drew some water for the horse to drink. The gears needed packing, but there hadn't been any grease left for me to do it with so I sat there and listened to it squawl in my ear while it worked.

When there was enough water in the tank I turned the machine off the way I had found it and climbed back down. The water was good to taste. I let the horse drink his fill and then quicklike stripped and crawled into the tank for a short bath. I felt a whole lot better afterward too.

I studied the situation some and decided I must have lost my way somehow even if that did seem impossible when I was following a railroad. I knew for sure that I wanted to ask somebody before I went any farther.

There were no buildings in view, but a road of sorts led east from the loading dock. The ruts were well packed, but I noticed that the center track was beginning to be weed-grown. The path was packed too hard still for grass to come in, but it looked like there had been little horse traffic along it for some time. Either it was being driven only with hitched pairs or was now being used mostly by trucks.

I pointed my gelding down the ruts and bumped him into that

road-eating jog that every good working horse should have. It was another six or seven miles to the buildings at the end of the road.

It was a fine collection of buildings too.

The corrals and working pens were stoutly built and well laid out, one leading into another and the gates set to swing into the runways to sort cattle into this pen or that. I liked the setup.

Beyond the pens there was a huge hay barn and past that a long, low machinery shed. The building I took to be a bunkhouse was bigger than most, and there was the usual assortment of small sheds and miscellaneous outbuildings. The house was a rambling two-story affair with shutters at the windows and climbing-rose-covered trellises flanking the front entry. It was really a pretty place.

Nice as it was, though, it needed some work. All the buildings were painted white with black trim, but the paint was aging and starting to flake. One of the shutters on the house had sagged, and the shingles on several of the outbuilding roofs, particularly on the big barn, were years beyond the need for replacement.

If anyone was at home I couldn't tell it from where I was, but that wasn't any way to judge. I'd stopped the horse kind of without thinking about it while I looked the place over. Now I nudged him forward again and rode the rest of the way in.

CHAPTER 4

The lady of the house was at home though it took a third knock on the back door to rouse her. When she did open it, it looked like she had been sleeping even though it was the middle of the day in the middle of the week. Her eyes certainly looked puffy underneath and her cheeks a bit flushed.

Aside from that she wasn't too bad to look at although she was far from being a beauty. She was a reasonably nice-looking, ordinary sort of woman. Not too tall and a little thin. Her hair was medium brown and was cropped short and just kind of left to fall the way it wanted without being pinned or twisted or curled. She was wearing a plaid dress that was mostly blue. It fitted loose and floppy and didn't reach within a foot of the floor although she was decently covered with dark stockings. Her eyes were probably her best feature, large and brown and glistening in spite of looking so reddened and puffy underneath. Most times I imagined her eyes would be real pretty.

She swung the door open and looked me up and down, and before I had a chance to ask any questions she began asking some, which was her right as it was her door this stranger had come rapping at.

"You're a cowboy, aren't you?" she wanted to know.

"Yes, ma'am," I said, pulling my hat off.

She looked me over again, more thoroughly this time, and said, "I haven't seen you around here before."

"I just got in, ma'am. Been working out east of here, the other side of Cheyenne Wells. Never been here before except passing through on the train."

She nodded as if that somehow satisfied her about something. "You know how to pull a calf?"

"Yes, ma'am, though it seems to me we never had to do it so much when I was a kid. But . . ." She cut me off with an impatient little wave of her hand before I could explain that I wasn't looking for work here, just for directions.

"I know, I know. I've heard it all before. These new breeds don't throw calves the way the old Spanish cattle used to. If I've heard that once, I've heard it a thousand times, but the fact is, a person has to deal with what he has and not what used to be. Right?"

"Yes, ma'am." Well, how could anybody argue with a statement like that?

"I'm not hiring," she went on. "Not regular hands I'm not. But I could use you for day wages, cowboy. A dollar fifty a day and found. Just for a few days, mind. I can't afford a regular hand right now. I won't try to deceive you. I'll pay you cash the end of each day for as long as I use you. All right?"

That wasn't what I'd come for, but shoot, if I went on into town, it would cost me that out of my savings for room and board while I was waiting to find out something about the Whiskey Ranch liquidation. Getting that amount on the plus side instead of the minus for a few days didn't sound too bad to me when I thought about it.

"I guess that would be all right, ma'am."

"All right then," she said. Very businesslike. She shoved a hand forward. "What's your name, cowboy?"

I grinned. "Cowboy."

"Come again?" She looked puzzled and seemed to have forgotten the hand she had just offered.

I took a soft hold on her fingertips and shook it briefly before I said, "That's what people call me, ma'am. Cowboy Russel. I've been known that way for a long time."

She smiled a little once her confusion was cleared up. "Good enough, Cowboy. I'm Mrs. Lacey." She hesitated for a moment, then stepped back from the door. "It's nearly dinner time. You haven't eaten?"

"No, ma'am . . . Miz Lacey . . . nor breakfast or supper either. And I thank you." I stepped inside and put my hat on the antler rack she indicated.

There was a small hand pump at the kitchen sink, probably drawing from a cistern judging by the size of it and the short, easy handle travel. She let me wash there while she put a meal together.

"I don't suppose you could butcher a beef for me," she asked when the dinner was ready. It was a meatless meal, and I supposed that her question was as much an apology as it was a request.

"I could do that," I assured her. "Should I find a steer or should I wait to see if there's a heifer goes down in calving?"

She gave me a brief, questioning look that she did not follow with words. What she said was, "You'd better wait to see the heifers first."

"Good. That's just the way it should be done."

This time her answering look was one of amusement. "Thank you, Cowboy. I'm glad you approve."

Which was a gentle enough way of putting me in my place. And, of course, she was right to do it. Making decisions—or approving those of others—really wasn't the business of a day-labor hand, but it was a bad habit that kept creeping up on me at times. It was a habit that I suppose I should have tried harder to break than was actually the case.

"If you would point me toward your calving ground, Miz Lacey . . . ?"

"Of course."

We left the table, where I had accomplished most of the eating that had been done, and she led me outside.

"The heifers are in a holding pasture about two miles north. You see that bluff up there? The gate is just southwest of that. You can put your things in the bunkhouse over there. I have a few head of horses in a pen the other side of the barn. Use any of them you like."

I guess I must have raised an eyebrow or something for she caught my question without me asking it.

"No, they aren't in anyone's string. I don't have any regular hands here at the moment." Her tone of voice was abrupt and businesslike when she said that, and it was perfectly clear that *why* she had no hands at the moment was none of my affair.

"Then I'll take my pick of the bunks, ma'am, and be on my way."

I led my horse from the house tie rail to the bunkhouse and moved my things inside.

The place was fairly large. It held fourteen bunks and had floor space for more. There weren't any blankets on any of the bunks, and the grass-stuffed mattresses were flat. The place needed some sweeping, which I would do later, but otherwise it wasn't bad. I dropped my gear onto the bunk nearest the stove and made a mental note of where a wall lamp was so I wouldn't have any trouble finding one when I got back.

The horses were where I was told. Just three of them, standing hipshot and sleepy in the sunshine. The appearance of my gelding brought their ears up, but they didn't seem to find the idea of having company very exciting.

I stripped the kack off my bay and hung it on a rail. When I turned him loose in the pen he rolled and shook and began working on the dusty hay in a rick nearby. He didn't show any more interest in the strangers than they showed in him.

I took my catch rope off my saddle and strolled across the hoof-softened floor of the corral, shaping a loop as I walked. My attention was still on those horses' ears, wondering how they were going to react to being caught and trying to decide which of the three would be the steadiest. I didn't want to walk back my first time out on this place, and I sure wouldn't need speed or spirit on a horse when I would be wallowing on the ground pulling calves.

It was when I got close to them and had decided to use a straight-shouldered grulla that I got the surprise.

Each of the three was branded on the right flank. With a big XXX. This place where I was working was the Whiskey.

CHAPTER 5

The grulla humped his back and tried me a few hops, but he wasn't serious about it. I pointed him toward the round-shouldered mesa Mrs. Lacey had pointed out to me and gave him enough rein that he could work off his confinement. When I pulled him back to a jog after five minutes or so I found that he had the rough, uncomfortable trot I expected from those entirely too vertical shoulder blades. I kneed him back up into a lope the rest of the way to the gate. At that gait his poor conformation wasn't so noticeable.

I did some thinking on the way. No wonder I had been riding so long without having to cross fences. The Whiskey was supposed to be a pretty good-sized place. And no wonder those handsome headquarters buildings were so empty and starting to need repair. A place that was in for a liquidation sale couldn't be in very good financial shape.

Mrs. Lacey probably thought I knew all about where I was and what was going on there. That was probably why she told me she would pay me each day instead of letting it build. In cash at that. It used to be that everybody paid off in cash, in hard coin at that, but these last few years the big outfits had mostly begun paying with paper, some of them with folding currency but a lot by check. That was almost expected now on a good-sized ranch. I was willing to bet, though, that no one was taking Whiskey checks anymore.

I couldn't help but wonder what had brought such a fine place to such a low state of affairs. The grass I was crossing now was about as good as any I had ever covered, and a prudent man can make a living even on poor ground. Certainly the water I had

had back at that tank had been good to drink and quick to rise when the mill began drawing. If he had both grass and water, a man shouldn't want for anything more.

There was no way I could know all the whys, of course. And again it really was not my affair. I should only be hoping that the Lacey misfortune would be my ticket to the future.

And did I want some of this land? Listen, I'd coveted the scrub grazing ground down in West Texas and that in the Panhandle. Compared to that, this rolling Colorado plains land was like the Garden of Eden. I wouldn't doubt that you could use a cow pen thirty acres here. Maybe fewer. Compared with what I had grown up on, that was no ground at all for a single cow.

This was fine country, there was no doubt about it, and I rode across it with a high degree of appreciation . . . and maybe anticipation. Maybe greed? I hope not. Some maybe. It really was fine country. I came to the wire gap that served as a gate and tucked my thoughts aside so I could pay attention to the job at hand.

The heifers were not in sight, but looking at the bob-wire fence that stretched out into the distance I began to suspect that this pasture was as big as some ranches I had worked on. I closed the gap behind me and remounted the grulla.

I found the stock within a half hour. There were three or four hundred head in the widely scattered herd. If all of these were first-calf heifers, the Whiskey was running beef on the old scale. I knew a good many fellows who made their living off fewer livestock than the Whiskey had first-calf heifers.

The calving was well along as I could see calves beside perhaps a quarter of the grown animals in the herd. Another quarter likely would have missed and would not drop calves this year. Some of the apparently dry heifers would have lost their calves, especially if there hadn't been anyone riding the bunch to help pull them out.

What I had told Mrs. Lacey at her back door had been quite literally true. The old-time Spanish cattle, or Texas cattle if you prefer, really hadn't needed any help at birthing. That was all we had owned when my father was in the business, and I doubt that he ever once pulled a calf in all the time he was running stock. I know it wasn't until I was out on my own working for wages that I learned how to do it.

These new breeds, though, with their big bodies and wide heads were a problem for birthing, and I'm not old enough to be prejudiced against them. I know they bring a better profit at slaughter, and so I am for them, in particular for the white face, which adapts so well to the plains' winters and stem-cured grasses. I am simply stating facts. The fact is that with modern stock you have to tend them close or often if you expect to keep your death losses down, both in calves and heifers.

Of those heifers walking around in the pasture now there would be a fair number that had borne dead calves. And scattered here and there would also be some dead heifers that would not live to increase the Whiskey herd.

These were good-looking, white face cattle spread out in front of me, and among them I could see a number of dark red bodies lying on the ground. Most of those would just be cattle lying down for a while. A few would be dead. Some of them would be heifers having trouble with their calving. It was these I had to find. I moved the grulla quietly among the herd.

Most of the heifers I approached got to their feet and lumbered out of my way. One that I passed had been dead for several days. A little farther on I found a heifer with a freckled face and sweat-darkened hide. She was too weak from long labor to do more than roll her eyes and feebly raise her head when I came near. I dismounted and hobbled the grulla as I did not yet know how surely he would ground too. Popular notions to the contrary, a ground tied horse is mostly a loose animal unless you are close enough to grab him when he starts to go.

I took my coat off and rolled my sleeves up. Within a few minutes I was wishing I had removed my shirt too. The calf had to be turned to meet the channel and even shoulder deep inside the heifer—too exhausted now to be afraid—I was having trouble getting it done. At least I wasn't too late to save this one if I could get it turned successfully. I could feel the unborn calf inside its sack, moving beneath my hand as I worked. I took a purchase on the ground with my boot heels and tried to force my arm a little deeper inside the heifer.

It was nearly dark when I left the heifer pasture and way past it when I got back to the Whiskey headquarters. I don't know what it is about that kind of work—shoot, I'd been lying down most of the time—but I was dead tired now.

Smelled pretty awful too. You can't spend that much time rooting around in a cow's innards without getting squirted every so often. So I was pretty nasty even after just a half-day's work.

I turned the grulla loose in the pen and hung my gear on a handy rail. The horse rolled and shook just like he'd been doing all the work. Show-off. He hadn't raised a decent sweat all afternoon.

With Mrs. Lacey apt to be somewhere around—someone had filled the hay rick while I was gone and from what I'd seen before it had to have been her who did it—I couldn't take a proper bath. I sure could wash up though.

There were troughs in the unused pens. I found one with some water in it and stripped my shirt off. I washed myself as well as I could and sloshed the worst of the gunk off my shirt too. I decided I'd have to wear my good shirt in the evenings and this nasty one while I was working, at least as long as I was pulling calves. I won't pretend that was a job I enjoyed, but it had to be done or the Laceys would lose beef.

I changed into cleaner stuff in the bunkhouse and turned the lamp down low before I walked across to the house. I knocked once and let myself into the kitchen.

Mrs. Lacey wasn't there but the lights were burning and I could see a fire still flickering in the stove. There was a coffeepot at the back of the range top. I checked. It was full. There was also a dinner of fried potatoes and cornmeal mush and fresh biscuits in the warming oven.

I hadn't exactly forgotten about butchering fresh meat during the afternoon, but none of the heifers I had been working with had died. I almost regretted that when I saw another meatless meal.

I set the food out on the table and had to hunt to find a plate and tableware. I guessed she had forgotten about that. I found a cup while I was at it. Boy, did that coffee taste good.

Mrs. Lacey came in as soon as I had sat down to eat. Once again she looked like she'd been asleep.

"Did I disturb you with my noise looking for things, Miz Lacey?"

"No, I . . . oh, I *am* sorry I forgot to set the table. I didn't know how long to wait supper for you. It was getting so late and . . ."

"Ah, that's okay." I tried some of the mush. It was better than it looked. Not a lot better, but . . .

"Before Jack . . . no, I mean, when we had a regular crew here, the hands were always in and ready to eat by sundown or a few minutes past."

"That's wasteful of good daylight, ma'am. A horse can always find his way home in the dark."

She gave me a small smile. "I like that attitude, Cowboy. There aren't many who have it anymore, I'm afraid."

"I can't believe that that's really so. Any good stockman hates waste. That's no different now than it was fifty years ago if a man wants to call himself a husbandman."

"And you, Cowboy? Do you call yourself that?"

"Yes I do, Miz Lacey."

"I don't think I ever heard a cowhand call himself a husbandman before. It isn't a common word. Not even among upper-crust stockmen."

"It's so just the same." I grinned at her. "Besides, maybe you haven't asked too many of them."

"No, maybe I haven't."

For some reason I could not begin to understand, she looked very sad and very lonely when she said that. I certainly hadn't thought I had gotten into any impolite or improper areas of discussion; most certainly hadn't meant to. The best thing would probably be to pretend I hadn't noticed, for sadness and hurt are very private things and not to be shared willy-nilly with strangers. I gave my attention to my plate.

Mrs. Lacey seemed to have caught some of my embarrassment or perhaps some of her own. She left the table and got herself some coffee and refilled my cup.

"How did you do today, Cowboy?" The lightness of her tone sounded a little bit forced, but not badly so.

"Three of them, ma'am. They all made it."

"That's wonderful." She seemed genuinely pleased that time.

I shrugged. "They prob'ly would have made it anyway." Which wasn't entirely true. One of them might have, the other two almost certainly would not have lived, and they might have lost one of the heifers too.

"That reminds me," she said. She left the room and came back a moment later. She put six quarters on the table beside my plate.

I shoved three of them aside. "You only got half a day's work. Fair is fair."

"You worked as much today as most of my hands have in a full day."

"Fair is fair," I repeated. I finished the meal and pocketed my three two-bit pieces. Fair was fair indeed, but Lord knew I had earned those quarters.

"I could rustle my own breakfast if you don't get up that early, ma'am," I told her as I rose and got my hat.

It was her turn to shake her head. "Fair is fair, Cowboy. What time do you want it ready?"

"Daylight is a little after six. Call it five-fifteen?"

"Very well. I'll have it waiting for you."

"Thank you, ma'am. Good night now."

"Good night, Cowboy."

CHAPTER 6

The woman was as good as her word. Breakfast was ready when I got over to the house, last night's mush sliced and fried and a generous platter of fried eggs and a fresh pot of coffee. At that hour of morning she didn't seem to much feel like conversation, but the truth was that she looked less like she'd been sleeping now than she had either time I'd seen her the day before.

There was still no sign of Mr. Lacey, but that wasn't entirely unreasonable. With the place in financial difficulties he might well be off visiting bankers here, there and everywhere trying to keep it floating. I know I would have been in his place. I know Pop had made the effort when our home was going.

I didn't say anything about his absence and she didn't offer. I got my breakfast down fast and used some bread and cooling eggs to make sandwiches for my dinner.

"I'll be back some time after dark," I told her.

She just nodded to tell me that would be all right.

The grulla had not been worked hard the afternoon before, but fair was fair as I had told the lady. I put my rope onto a heavy-boned sorrel and had to fight the saddle onto his back and fight him again to get him to take the bit. He was rank enough that I would have bet it was a long time since he'd been ridden, so I topped him the first time inside the corral where I could be sure of catching him again if he unloaded me.

I guess there are some fellows who will brag that they've never been thrown, and I suppose it just could be that some of them are telling the truth. I have noticed, though, that I have never heard a man or a boy say that while he was sitting on a horse. Nor have I ever ridden with anyone that wondrous good. As for myself, I freely admit that the horse will win from time to time. The idea is to win the wars even if you can't win all the battles.

I got onto that big sorrel and made sure my seat was deep and snug before I ever turned loose of the cheek-strap. As soon as he had his head he went to work on me, and a fine job he did of it too. I was breathing dust in no time at all. A few jumps more and I was tasting it. I got up and brushed myself off and went to fetch my rope so I could catch him again.

This time I rigged a bucking roll across my pommel by rolling my slicker into a tight sausage roll and tying it there. I took a tight grip on the horn and tried him again. This time I lasted nearly a full minute, I judge, before he caught me leaning in anticipation of what I thought he was going to do, and he ducked out the other way.

I caught him the third time and jumped back astraddle him. By now he was sweating heavy and starting to tire. This time I finally was able to ride him down into a walk. Just to be on the safe side I loped him around the pen in tight circles until the nervousness was worked out of him. Only then would I trust him outside. Once he was ridden down, though, he proved to be a good horse and I was pleased with him.

By then, though, it was coming daylight so that I would be wasting Whiskey sunshine just getting to the heifer pasture. I put the sorrel into an easy run toward the wire gap and let him make up for some of the time he had cost me.

It was a fine, clear morning, warming as soon as the sun was properly into the sky, and I suppose it just could be that those heifers thought it entirely too fine a day to ruin as I found none of them in any great difficulty. Most of the morning turned out to be no more than a slow and lazy ride through the young Whiskey herd. I did find one strapping big red heifer that looked like she was having trouble, but she convinced me otherwise and dropped her calf just fine without my help.

Late morning I did find one in trouble, but I wasn't able to earn my pay there either. The calf was already dead inside her and she couldn't get rid of it. I tried for several hours to help her, but ended up having to take it out in pieces.

It was past lunch time by then so I rode over to the clay-lined tank full of the melt runoff at this time of year and washed myself and ate my sandwiches. By the time I got back to the heifer she was dead, as I had expected, so I used the horse to drag her into a downhill position and bled her out. Later in the afternoon I came back and butchered some fresh meat that I hoped Mrs. Lacey would be willing to burn for our supper. It had been entirely too long since I'd had meat. The rest of the carcass I opened up to cool, thinking if the coyotes and foxes didn't do too much damage overnight I could carry the rest back the next day.

When I got back that evening I had lost that one calf and its mama and had saved only one other calf to make up for it. It was not a good day's work.

Mrs. Lacey was not upset when I told her, though. If I hadn't been there she would have lost more than she actually did. And I guess it had been a while since she had had beef too.

"How would you like this fixed, Cowboy?"

"Why, the best way, ma'am. Drenched in tallow and fried till it looks like leather."

She smiled. "I used to fix it that way for my daddy all the time. It was his favorite too."

"Then I would have to say that your daddy was a sensible man, Miz Lacey. Old-time cowman was he?"

"Yes, why do you ask?"

"Because I don't think I ever met one of that breed who wasn't partial to tallow-fried steak and hot biscuits."

Her good humor faded. "You may be right." She sighed. "My husband likes his meat boiled."

There wasn't anything polite I could say to that so I backed out of the conversation. "If you'll excuse me then, ma'am, I'll go wash and change to a clean shirt."

"Of course, Cowboy." She smiled again. "It will be ready when you get back."

I took my time about cleaning up and putting on my good

shirt. It takes some time to properly cook a slab of meat, and I was not altogether comfortable with Mrs. Lacey. I couldn't entirely figure out her and her moods and problems, although a lot of it would certainly have to do with the Whiskey's financial troubles.

You know, it is a funny thing but I was beginning to have some mixed feelings about that myself. I mean, I had come to this part of the country strictly because of the liquidation. The possibility of my getting a piece of Whiskey land on the cheap was my best shot at having a place of my own any time in the near future. My future success might very well be a direct result of their failure.

On the other hand, I just couldn't help but think how I would feel in their place. I could remember very well how things had been for Pop and us when we were going through the same thing. It was not something one person would wish onto another who had done him no harm.

And, too, I was riding for the Whiskey Brand myself now. It was just day labor it was true, but it was their food I had in my belly, and I had some of their money in my pocket. A man who wants to hold a high opinion of himself can't very well wish his employer ill.

So I was kind of pulled two ways about the Whiskey.

I put it out of mind for the moment. Right now there was tallow-fried steak to be thinking about.

The meal was ready and, Lord, it did taste good after being so long without meat. I made my way through enough for several people.

"I do like to see a man enjoy a meal like that, Cowboy. It makes a body feel like she's done something good by cooking it." She got a wistful look to her. "That was the way I used to feel about cooking for my daddy."

"It sounds like you were pretty close to your dad."

"I was."

"That's mighty nice, Miz Lacey. I . . . uh . . . take it you lost him?"

"Two years ago."

"Was he from around here?"

She gave me an odd sort of look. "My father was Joshua Turnbull."

"Yes, ma'am?" I waited for her to go on but she didn't.

"That doesn't mean anything to you, does it?" She sounded curious about that.

"No, ma'am. Should it?"

"My father was Joshua Turnbull. *His* father was Randall Turnbull. Grandpap founded the Triple-X back in 'seventy when there wasn't anything much here except antelope and Indians and maybe sixty or seventy white men down at Colorado City. He got most of it with agricultural college land scrip, the rest from the government. It was all open land then. A dollar and a quarter an acre for the government land. The scrip didn't cost anywhere near that. He built it from nothing, then he went back east to Illinois and married grandma. I never met her, but I remember him from when I was wee small. He had huge, white moustaches that tickled whenever he kissed me. I was sure he was 'way over a hundred years old then, but really he couldn't have been more than seventy-something." She stopped and I thought she had run out of breath. "*Why* am I telling you all this?" She sounded downright exasperated.

I couldn't help but laugh, and I don't think she took it unkindly. It certainly was not meant to be.

"It could be you just want to," I told her. "Has it been a while since you've had a chance to talk?"

"Yes-s-s," she said slowly. "I suppose it has been."

"Well, that's it then. You just needed an ear to pour something into. No big deal." I laughed. "Shucks, Miz Lacey, this way when your husband gets home you won't have to talk his ear off."

I intended that as a joke, not as an invasion of privacy, but she certainly took it seriously.

"Mr. Lacey will not return, I think." Her voice turned bitter. "He might be asked to repay some of the money he took when he left. Bastard."

Modern times or no modern times, that was strong language for a lady to use. I think it unnerved her too for she left the table and spent longer than necessary filling coffee cups that were still half full from the last time.

"I didn't mean . . ."

"I know," she said before I could finish. She made a braying, snorting sort of sound that probably was intended to be a laugh. "You certainly were right, Mr. Russel. Apparently I have been needing an ear to bend. I'm sorry if I . . ."

"It's fine, ma'am. No problem. I'm a good listener." I grinned. "Besides, I don't know a soul around here to repeat gossip to. So feel free any time you want to talk. Or need to."

I said the words, and I meant them too, but even meaning it didn't take away the bit of discomfort I was feeling. I had a feeling that I was treading where I did not belong. I drained off my coffee though it was still much too hot for that after the refilling.

"Was there anything else, Miz Lacey?"

"No, nothing. Thank you, Cowboy."

"Any time, ma'am. Really." I got my hat and headed for the comfort of my bunk.

CHAPTER 7

"I forgot to give you your pay last night," she said. "I'm sorry."

"Heck, I forgot it too." She had laid six quarters beside my plate at the breakfast table. I put them into my pocket and sat down.

"Miz Lacey, you really ought to be getting more for your money if there's no heifers having trouble. A body never knows about that. Is there something else I could be doing out that way? Just in case?"

"Oh my, Cowboy, there must be a thousand things to do if I just had the men and the time to get them done." She sat my plate in front of me and brought only a cup of coffee for herself. She took a chair near mine and said, "Most of the crew was laid off a month and a half ago. There really hasn't been anything done since then. And the truth is that I grew up right here, but I don't know all that much about the management of a ranch. I can play piano and show a lively dimple all the while. I can take my hunter over four rails or a bramble hedge. I can twirl a parasol with the very best of them. But I know very little about cattle or finances."

"Then it could be that this is the time to start learning, ma'am."

She made a face. "I've been receiving a crash course these past two months. What I have learned so far is that it is too late to undo the damage Jack managed to do when he left."

She seemed to still have some talking she wanted to do. "Two months, you said," I prompted her. It was like pulling the board in a floodgate.

"Two months since Jack left. That was the end of it, though,

really. The beginning was two years ago when Daddy died. My
mother passed away when I was twelve. I never had any brothers
or sisters. Daddy had one brother, but he died during the war
with the Spanish."

"Cuba?" I asked. Everyone from South Texas to northern
North Dakota still talked about Cuba and The Colonel. The
Great War had done nothing to diminish that.

Mrs. Lacey made a small sound that seemed to be part remembered fondness and part amusement. "Uncle Carl never was
very dramatic. He was the quiet one of the family I'm told, although all I remember about him was sitting in his lap before he
left. His uniform coat was scratchy. Anyway, no. He never got to
Cuba. He got sick on the trains and died in a place called Port
Tampa.

"When Daddy died I was the last of the Turnbulls. A very
good catch, some apparently thought. Jack did.

"We had a good crew then—Daddy always did—and a marvelous foreman. Daddy's lawyers took care of all the paperwork, so
I really wasn't needed for anything. Some friends down in the
city had me come stay with them. A girl I went to school with
and her family. I was there nearly six months.

"After a while they started taking me out in public occa-
sionally. We went to the polo matches at The Broadmoor one
day. You know what that is, don't you?"

I nodded. It was a rich man's way of letting his horses exercise
for him while he used a stick to swat a ball through some
goalposts. Not that it was anything to complain about. Since the
players were, after all, some very wealthy fellows, they didn't
much care what they paid for their horses. I helped a man up in
Nebraska train and deliver ten head to a broker in Omaha. They
were undersized geldings too small for roping or hard ranch
work and should have been worth twenty dollars or so even when
the British were buying horses so heavily. If I remembered correctly the broker paid two hundred apiece for them. And that
was for resale. The man in Omaha certainly allowed himself

plenty of room for profit. Anyway, yes, I knew something about polo.

"That was where I met Jack," she said. "He was a cadet then and very dashing in his uniform after the matches. He cut quite a handsome figure during the games as well. He was from the East, here with the VMI team on a polo and recruiting tour. He was a senior that year, upperclassman I believe they called it, and was expecting to be called up and commissioned in the cavalry when he graduated. It turned out that he was rejected for service—he was always a little vague about why he was turned down.

"In any event, he was a most dashing and correct gentleman, or so he seemed at the time." She hesitated. "Jack is several years younger than I." She said that almost apologetically.

"He asked permission to call on me at my friend's home. Later we corresponded. That went on until he graduated the following spring. He wrote and told me he wouldn't be going into the service. His letter sounded . . . so dispirited, so at loose ends. I wrote back and invited him to visit me here. I was living at home again by then. And I was getting lonely too, to tell the truth. The only men who came calling—some of them *quite* old too—were so *obvious* about wanting Daddy's land. They scarcely bothered to differentiate between the daughter and the gatepost. My girl-friends were mostly married, and it is a long drive out from the city.

"Jack wasn't like the others. Not in the slightest." She made a face. "I imagine he found me to be quite the country bumpkin. And I suppose he was right. He had intended a month's visit, or so he said when he arrived. At the end of the month he asked for my hand. I was flattered. Not merely by the proposal but by his attentions during my loneliness. I accepted. We were married five weeks later in the little Episcopal Church in Monument. It was a small ceremony. Very private.

"My foreman left shortly thereafter. Jack said he had accepted a manager's position in Montana. I thought it odd that he would leave without discussing it with me—he had been with us six years—but I only thought it rude, not significant. Jack took over management of the Triple-X.

"Jack became very involved in the business of the ranch. He read countless bulletins on beef production and bloodline upgrading. I know he did a great deal of conferring with our bankers in the city and with bankers and a law firm in Chicago. He made several trips to Chicago, he said to look at some purebred bulls for herd improvement. I'm guessing about the Chicago bankers because of letterhead printing on correspondence Jack received here afterward. The law firm I am certain about. He didn't pay them, you see. They dunned *me* for his bill *after* he left." She sounded downright indignant about that.

I got up and poured coffee for both of us while she got over being mad.

"What he had done," she went on, "was to take out mortgages against nearly all of the Triple-X livestock. He did buy some bulls and a few seed cows while he was back East, but he got them all on credit.

"Craig Rundelman at my bank told me that Jack even approached him about mortgaging the Triple-X itself. The only reason he did not do that, apparently, was that the property mortgage would have required my signature." She mocked herself with a short, bitter bark of laughter. "What dear Jack did not know was that I trusted him so completely I most probably would have signed a property mortgage if he had told me it was necessary. Then he really *would* have been well set when he walked away from me." She sighed.

"The laws governing a woman's property being what they are, though, Jack was able to pledge Triple-X livestock against loans on his signature alone. As soon as he had our full book count under mortgage, he made one last gesture. He shipped for slaughter our herd of two-year-old steers on winter pasture— although they too were under mortgage—and pocketed the money for them. He collected the check from the buyer and apparently flagged the next passenger cars coming through. The hands told me he had stayed behind, in any event, when the load-

ing was done. His horse was found still in the siding stock pens
the next day, so the reasonable presumption is that he took the
late southbound coach to Santa Fe.

"At first I was worried about his safety, though. The hands
spent days searching for him. Then I received a rather stern note
saying the ranch accounts were overdrawn at the bank. There
should have been . . . quite a lot there. It was all gone. The
truth began to come out then, by dibs and dabs. I still don't know
for sure if I have all of it. Daddy's lawyer is still trying to put it
all together for me. He doesn't know if he will be paid for his
services."

She brightened somewhat, and it seemed only a little forced.
"And *that,* Mr. Russel, is my sad story for the day. I'm sorry
about keeping you from your work." She paused. "But thank you
for listening. I think it helped."

I was obviously being dismissed, which was just as well, considering. As it was, I was past daylight getting away from the
place.

CHAPTER 8

I spent a few more days baby-sitting the Whiskey heifers, but I really wasn't accomplishing all that much. There were not enough of them having problems at any given time to justify my pay, and there were no other Whiskey cows close to the pasture that I could be working in the meantime. I repacked a few windmills, including the one down at the loading pens where I also fixed the chain trip, but after a couple days of that I told Mrs. Lacey I thought she was wasting her money.

"I'd really rather you stay, Cowboy. I . . . think I may be needing a hand. I mean, one never knows about these things, does one?"

That was what she said, but the wide-open look of her eyes and the sudden tightening around her mouth said more. If I'd had to guess, I would have said that Mrs. Lacey was just plain lonely and maybe a little bit afraid of being out here on all this empty ground by herself. I suspect that as an old family debutante of the first water she never would have spent much time by her lonesome.

"Look," I told her, "you really are wasting your money paying me every day like you've been, but you're right that you might well need more help with those heifers. Why don't I ride into town for a day or two and then come back out here."

"You'll really come back?"

"I'll give you my promise on it, Miz Lacey."

"All right then." She sounded relieved. I got the impression she could manage just fine by herself so long as she knew it wasn't a permanent loneliness she faced.

I got directions from her on how I could reach Monument

from Whiskey Ranch—she offered the use of the ranch truck, but I wouldn't have known how to operate it—and I left early the next morning.

Monument turned out to be, well, not very big. It had a town hall and a couple stores and a couple churches and a couple blind pigs that pretended to be ordinary houses. There didn't seem to be a regular hotel in the town, but a number of private residences had new-looking signs out front saying they took boarders.

For a town that size there seemed to be a good many people about, most of them congregating in the vicinity of a combination drugstore and cafe, so that was where I went first. I noticed that I only saw two teams of horses on the streets, most of the traffic being gasoline driven. I tied my horse close enough to a Paige touring car that he could kick it if he wanted to.

The cafe part of the store was crowded even in midmorning. Most of the men were wearing business suits and narrow-brimmed Stetsons that looked out of place on Eastern-looking heads. Their owners were drinking coffee and eating doughnuts for the most part, and most of them were talking too loud to make themselves heard over the next fellow's too-loud talk. I found an empty chair at one of the quieter tables and took it.

"You boys don't mind some company, do you?" I asked.

There were three of them already at the table. Or two of them plus a third man, I quickly decided. The two who seemed to be together were a heavy, middle-aged man in a dark suit and matching vest with a gold chain and elk's tooth stretched across his belly, and a big, well set up man in a much less expensive suit who I judged was somewhere in his thirties or very early forties. That one looked like he could handle himself in a tight spot despite his city clothes. Put him in rough clothes and he could have passed for a hand. Or for a Tom Horn type range detective.

The third man was closer in appearance to the first. He was probably in his fifties and going gray, and his vest was beginning to have a little trouble containing his paunch. His cheeks were hidden by Burnside whiskers and his moustache was enough to give glory to a billygoat. He had an air about him, very quietly so, of being comfortable with very large chunks of money.

When I first sat down the big fellow, who was the youngest of them, gave me the start of a scowl that he quickly covered over when the third man, who was seated across the table from him, nodded and spoke a welcome.

"Of course you may join us," the gentleman said. He smiled and added, "It's entirely too crowded for formalities." The man offered his hand and introduced himself as Curtis Abelard of Chicago, Illinois.

The other well-dressed man was just as quick to give me his name then. He said he was Mel Tyler. He didn't say where he was from.

The last of them, the big young one, made no move to introduce himself although he did nod. Tyler supplied the information for him.

"My friend here," Tyler said, "is Henry Lonahan, my . . . companion."

That pause was deliberate, too, and no doubt about it. Companion, my foot. Lonahan was Tyler's bodyguard, which was what Tyler was so smugly telling even to total strangers. Which made me wonder what was so special about Tyler that he would need a bodyguard. Which might, after all, have been his whole point in getting that information out in such an oblique way.

Sure I had heard of Lonahan, though. Long Hands people sometimes called him. Long rifle was more like it. My first thoughts about the man, connecting him with the likes of old Tom Horn, had been right on the button, although Lonahan was neither so well known nor so flamboyant as Horn had been in his time.

A lot of things were said about Henry Lonahan, one of them being that he had gone to visit Horn in jail while that gentleman was waiting to be hanged and that Lonahan had studied under the man during Horn's imprisonment the way other eager pupils must once have studied under Socrates while the great philosopher waited for the hemlock. And for the same reason. The pupil wanted to learn to ape the master.

Well, maybe Lonahan hadn't gotten as good as his master had been, but everything you heard about the man pointed to his being one bad fellow to get crossways of. He was one of those who walks on the shady side of the law though always marginally connected with it. I know he was a livestock protective man for a while up in Nebraska because a buddy of mine knew him there. Before that, my buddy said, he had worked in Wyoming and Arizona.

Unlike Horn I had never heard of him actually murdering a white man. All the boys he had arrested—at least those that anyone knew about—had been hauled in for court trial although they were frequently in a pretty battered condition by the time they reached the hands of the regular law.

The last I had heard about Lonahan had been when I was over in Kansas, and all the talk among the younger boys was how much money they could make from roughnecking in the new oil fields down in eastern Oklahoma. A lot of that country was still owned by Indians, and I guess a lot of them were both pretty stubborn and pretty stupid about letting the oil explorers drill in their ground. I heard that Lonahan was hired as a specialist to help convince the reluctant ones that they should let drillers past their fences. Rumor had it that Lonahan was even meaner to Indians than he was with white men.

At any rate I pretended that I didn't tumble to the name and that I hadn't caught that "companion" business that Tyler was throwing around. I didn't want anything to do with a pair like that.

An overworked little waitress with practically no meat on her except at chest level, where she was downright oversize, came and asked if I wanted breakfast or just a snack. I told her it would be breakfast and set about thinking what it should be.

"We're too busy to cook things special," she said quickly. "If you want breakfast it's eggs, hotcakes and ham for fifty cents. If you don't want that it's coffee and a pair of crullers for a dime.

Take your pick." She sounded in a hurry. And as if she had said it all before.

I gave her a grin and a wink and took my time about drawling, "Oh-h-h, I think I'll have, uh, a breakfast there, li'l miss. And mind you take your time about bringing it, hear."

That brought a flutter of a smile and, "Now that's a switch, mister."

I gave her another wink and watched her walk away at a slightly slower pace than she had arrived at. She wasn't nearly as interesting from that angle but, heck, nobody can have everything.

Lonahan was watching her too. When she disappeared into the kitchen he turned and said to no one in particular, "There's a whole lot to some parts of that little thing, ain't there."

Hell, he made just looking at that little gal seem dirty, and from his tone of voice I got the idea that anything she wanted or didn't want would have no bearing on what he might choose to do.

Now I'm no prude, damnit. Far from that. But I do believe that a man ought to respect his lady friends or he has no business taking the pleasure of their company.

I didn't say anything and neither did Mr. Abelard. Tyler laughed a little.

The girl brought my meal and after riding already for some hours I was ready for it. I put it down in short order while the others exchanged pleasantries about weather and water and such.

When I was done I pushed my plate back and thanked Mr. Abelard and Tyler for their courtesy in such a way that Lonahan could assume he had been included if he wanted to.

The waitress was clearing off a table nearer the door. I took her aside and gave her sixty cents and said, "Miss, I know this is forward of me an' maybe you don't like to have anything to do with cowboys when the town's full of these fancy fellows, but . . . what I'm saying is, I'd sure enjoy your company when you get off work here."

I believe she took the suggestion kindly for she perked up considerable and gave me a real nice smile.

"I'm through at two o'clock," she said, "as soon as the heavy lunch trade is past. I could meet you at the door around back."

"I'll be looking forward to that, Miss . . . ?"

The smile got bigger. "Linda Matson."

"I'll be looking forward to it then, Linda."

I hired a driving rig and bought the makings for a picnic, and after two o'clock we drove south and west onto the side of the Front Range above a tidy little place she said was the Hay Creek Ranch until we found a little promontory where we could see the mountains behind and the plains below.

She turned out to be an awfully nice girl and good company, and I got her back to town in plenty of time for her to change and report back for work the next morning and with a date to meet me again when she got off.

We hadn't seen Lonahan anywhere, and of course I had not mentioned him to her. She was much too nice a girl to be bothered by the likes of him.

CHAPTER 9

I slipped Linda back into town quite a bit earlier that evening, shortly after dark, because she was plenty tired. She was still game for more picnicking, but I could see how bushed she was and took her on home. There was always another day tomorrow, I reminded her.

What happened, though, was that I found myself in town about nine-thirty, plenty of evening to go yet and nothing in particular to do.

The regular stores were closed so I turned the hired rig back to its owner and drifted over to one of the blind pigs I had noticed before.

The place was making a *very* thinly disguised attempt to look like somebody's home. It was in a house, it was true, but the place was blazing with electric lights, and you could hear the Victrola music blaring all the way out to the street. The front yard looked like a parking lot with its collection of fine automobiles and run-down flivvers and a lone mule-drawn farm wagon.

Since this or another just like it seemed to be the only games in town at this time of night, I looked it over, braced myself against the noise and went on in.

The sound of the music was scratchy and tinny and so loud I could feel it as much as hear it. There was an old boy propped lazily in a straight-back chair beside the door. He was wearing clodhopper shoes and dirty trousers and an undershirt and was chewing on a match stem. He didn't look like much, but I don't doubt at all that if I hadn't passed his inspection he would have come down all over me like two ton of fertilizer on a one-ton truck.

Instead he nodded and scratched himself and inclined his head toward the rooms deeper inside the house.

The big main room was filled with tables and men and a couple gaudy, bawdy women. It smelled of sweat and gin and blue tobacco smoke. That much was all right, but this was where they had set the Victrola and at such close quarters that was a bit too much for comfort. I went into a smaller room off to the side where the sound wasn't quite so big.

This room must have been a study or a library at one time. It was pine paneled and almost dark in spite of the wall-mounted electric bulbs. Instead of tables, this room was filled with leather-covered overstuffed chairs and little game tables just big enough to hold a checker board. There weren't so many people here either.

There were a couple men bent over a chess game and another man who was slumped deep into his chair. That one was snoring softly. He had an empty glass and a large, wet stain in his lap and the most peaceable, pleasant expression on his face. Just from looking at him I decided that he was a mighty nice fellow, and if I knew him I would like him.

"Mr. Russel."

I didn't see who it was at first.

"Back here."

I spotted a waving hand and then the man's face. It was Mr. Abelard, one of the men I'd had breakfast with the day before. He was sitting in a chair that had been pulled around to face out a window instead of into the room. I joined him there and he motioned me to drag a chair next to his.

"Evening, sir. I'm flattered you remember me."

"Of course I do, Mr. Russel. You should not underestimate yourself." He smiled. "Beside, I have good reason to remember you. Would you like to knock off Canadian—or rye perhaps?"

I shook my head.

"Wine then. They have a surprising selection here."

"I'm not much of a drinking man, Mr. Abelard. Look, uh, what was that about having a reason to remember me?"

"If you won't have something alcoholic, Mr. Russel, perhaps you'd like a soft drink. Or a cup of coffee." From the hint of amusement crinkling the corners of his eyes I could see he was having a bit of fun with me.

All right, I thought. "Coffee, then."

Mr. Abelard motioned with his left hand, without ever turning away from the window we were facing, and almost before he could drop his hand back to the arm of the chair there was a woman beside him to take his order. Shoot, I could've done that continuously until midnight and not accomplished anything except to make people wonder if the place was being infested with house flies. "A carafe of coffee, please, and another split of the champagne, dear."

It was delivered in no time at all, too. A small bottle of wine for Mr. Abelard and a whole pot of coffee just for me.

"Now," he said contentedly when we were both settled with our beverages, "where were we?"

"You were saying something about why you remembered me," I prompted.

"Yes, of course." The old boy remembered that quite well I was sure. "Do you recall Mr. Tyler?"

"Yes, sir."

"Of course, well, I had dinner this noon with Mr. Tyler and his secretary Mr. . . . um . . . Lanahan."

"Lonahan," I corrected automatically. "Did you say secretary?"

He shrugged. "Secretary, chauffeur, gentleman's gentleman . . ." That one he laughed at a bit. Neither of them seemed much of a gentleman even to me. "Whatever you want to call him."

"They aren't friends of yours, Mr. Abelard?"

He hesitated. I'm sure he would not want to say anything derogatory about either of them, but . . . "Acquaintances would be a better way to put it." He smiled faintly, as if to himself. "Mr. Tyler would like me to join him in a business venture of sorts."

I laughed and saluted him with my coffee cup. "A division of labor, perhaps? His acumen and your capitalization?"

He laughed right out loud at that, but when he looked back at me I thought it was with somewhat more respect. He had been friendly right along, of course, but I got the distinct impression that he now regarded me in a different light.

"I won't even ask you why you thought that," he said, still chuckling, "but it would not be proper for me to confirm your guess, Mr. Russel. And I believe we managed to sidetrack ourselves there."

"Sorry," I said with a grin. I really liked this Mr. Abelard, and he really was the gentleman that Henry Lonahan nor no man who ever hired him could hope to be.

"As I started to say, I had lunch with them today, and Mr. Lonahan grumbled through most of the meal. He kept looking at the girl who was waiting on us and complaining about that, if I may use his words, that 'damned cowboy' who was beating his time. I take it you had the pleasure of the young lady's company, Mr. Russel?"

"She's a delightful girl," I said.

He looked at me closely for a moment. "Lonahan was saying she never returned to her boardinghouse last night."

That was not a comment I would have expected from a gentleman like Mr. Abelard, but I didn't let it throw me. "Perhaps she chose to spend the night with a friend," I said as smooth as oil, which was not exactly a lie either. "And perhaps Mr. Lonahan should be careful of slandering a kind and gentle girl who has done him no harm."

Abelard nodded his approval. "I agree, Mr. Russel, or I would not have repeated the comment, believe me."

"I do, sir."

"Thank you. And if I may repeat one thing more, I received a strong impression that Mr. Lonahan intends this evening to press his attentions on the young lady."

I set my cup aside.

"Mr. Russel," he added, before I could speak, "the girl has

served me several times in the past week. I have always found her
to be efficient and, moreover, pleasant beyond the necessity of
her occupation. I would not wish her anything but well."

"Nor would I, Mr. Abelard. Now if you will excuse me, sir, I
think I will take a little walk in the night air. It's supposed to be
good for the health I'm told. Thank you for the coffee." I stood to
leave.

Abelard smiled. "If I were a little younger I would walk with
you, Mr. Russel. Take care you don't stumble in the darkness."

"I will, Mr. Abelard. Good night, now."

He smiled and nodded and took a small sip of his champagne.
He looked very much like a satisfied old Tom cat with ancient
battle scars on his hide and a telltale sign of feathers fringing his
mouth. He had taken our conversation exactly where he wanted
it to go.

Well, that was just fine with me. I don't at all mind being used
so long as I know that I am and happen to agree with the
manipulator's objects. In this case I certainly did agree.

I left the noise of the speakeasy behind and ambled through
the shadows on my way back to Linda's place.

She lived on the second story of a frame roominghouse near
the railroad tracks. I had not been inside her room, of course, but
I knew which it was and that she reached it by way of an outside
staircase on the side of the house. That was where I had had to
leave her both times I brought her home. Her window was dark
behind a lowered shade, and I was sure she would be sleeping
soundly by now. It would be a great pity if anyone disturbed her
sleep. Or worse.

I took a good look around in the side yard of the boardinghouse and chose a dark spot under a bush at the foot of the
stairs where I could make myself comfortable. I settled in there
and sat about thinking some pleasant thoughts and spinning
some happy daydreams while I waited.

After a while, say two or two and a half hours, Mr. Lonahan
came to call on Miss Linda. Judging from his stiff-legged gait I
would say that he was carrying a pretty heavy load. He took hold

of the bannister rail, burped once and paused for a moment to steady himself.

Now I will tell you a truth about myself. There is not a hell of a lot that I am scared of, but I have never been one to believe, either, that pride should be allowed to lead to foolishness. Put a little more plainly, that philosophy could translate to: If you have some doubts about winning fair, find a better way to do it.

I picked up the length of two-by-four I had had the foresight to provide for myself, stepped up behind Mr. Henry Lonahan and laid a two-handed whack across the gentleman's head and shoulders.

After ten or fifteen minutes of tidying up—he was big enough to be quite a handful for one person to manage—I went over to the barn where I'd left my horse and crawled into their straw pile for a good night's sleep.

The last I saw of Mr. Lonahan he was in a deep and peaceful sleep himself.

CHAPTER 10

I didn't see Mr. Abelard the next morning—or Mr. Lonahan—but I did see Linda Matson. We drove up to a place called Palmer Lake and watched several groups of excursionists playing croquet and lawn tennis in the sunshine. It was a lovely day and a lovelier time we had, and she promised me she would stay with a girlfriend for a few days just in case Lonahan was not yet discouraged.

I dropped her at the friend's house quite late and as I was not really that tired exchanged the hired rig for my own horse and headed him back toward the Whiskey. It was time I got out of that town, I decided.

I was there in plenty of time to be rapping on the kitchen door at five-fifteen. Darned if Mrs. Lacey didn't have breakfast ready enough for two.

"You don't look any worse for wear," she said.

"Oh, I'm not much for drinking." I poured the coffee while she put the food out.

"Were there . . . many people there?" she asked.

"Plenty." I loaded my plate with biscuits and began ladling gravy over them. "Lots of money in there right now. And a lot more that are trying to pretend they have it. Big cars and business suits everywhere you look."

"Vultures," she said. "No, worse than that. At least vultures wait until something is dead before they tear it apart. At least vultures are only trying to keep themselves alive. Those . . . *people*," she spit the word out, "are more like coyotes in a chicken roost, dragging living things down just for the smell of the blood."

"Some of them," I said.

"*All* of them," she said.

"Some of them," I repeated in a mild tone. I was thinking of Mr. Abelard. I would have to be pretty upset to think ill of him. But then I guess Mrs. Lacey was pretty upset.

She put all of her attention into her plate then, apparently unwilling to either agree with me or argue the point further. I finished my meal and thanked her and slid out quietly.

The table talk had left me in a mood for a bit of a workout, so I earred down and saddled the scrappy, big sorrel horse that had fought me before. This time though, he gave up after a minute or two and never did get serious enough to dump me off. That little excitement was practically disappointing, so I laid the steel to him and made him show me some speed all the way out to the heifer pasture. With all that crisp morning air in my face I felt a good bit better by the time I got there.

Nothing much had changed in the few days I'd been gone. I found one stillborn calf, which I might or might not have saved if I had been there, and several more of the young mothers in trouble that I was in time to help.

That night I told Mrs. Lacey, "Look, this being out there each and every day in one little pasture is a bad waste of your money, ma'am, and it's too far from town to make day-on, day-off work worth my time an' trouble. I spent some time studying on this today, and here's what I thought. It's up to you, of course, but what I'd suggest is that I spend one day with the heifers and the next out on your fences or with the rest of the stock. I think I could do more for you that way and not feel like I'm being a liability for you."

"Let me think about that awhile."

"Of course." I had already made up my mind, though. I hadn't come here in search of a job and was doing it just to be marking time, really. Rather than take her money to no purpose, I could just as easy move in closer to town and closer to Linda Matson. There were several beef operations much closer in where I might get work and at least could hit for a bunk and a grub-line hand-out.

After the meal she disappeared for a minute and again came back to the kitchen with six quarters for my pay.

"Miz Lacey, I just got to ask you this. How come you always pay me off with quarters?" I mean, seeing nothing but quarters for pay was an almighty curious thing.

She looked embarrassed and ducked her eyes away from mine. "I haven't had a chance to get to the bank recently. I happened to have some quarters on hand."

It dawned on me then what she really meant. "Do you mean, ma'am, that I've been robbing your piggy bank?"

I could see in her eyes that it was true.

"You're being paid in U.S. currency. Beyond that shouldn't concern you."

"Yes, ma'am." I certainly hadn't meant to rub into her the depths of her circumstances, but it was equally true that I was on the verge of heading for town. I took another look into those eyes, though, and I had a strong feeling that she knew what was in my thoughts.

There was fear in those eyes and loneliness. As uncomfortable as I was in taking what might have been her last handful of coins, my discomfort would have been all the worse if I sat comfortably in town knowing her pain and remembering I turned her down when I could have eased it. The woman had me boxed in whether she knew it or whether she did not.

"Which direction did you decide I should ride in the morning?" I asked.

She looked relieved, which was what I had intended. She knew I wasn't leaving right away.

"I'll accept your judgment, Cowboy." She was making a concession to match mine, I thought. "Tomorrow I would like you to ride east to the fence line and circle to the south checking fence and any stock you find."

"Surely I couldn't ride the whole of the Whiskey fence line in one day."

"No, but you could spend one night out and come back up the rails when you reach them."

"That sounds good, ma'am."

"I'll make up a sack of food for you to carry. Will you need anything else?"

"No. Nothing."

She nodded briskly. "In that event, I will see you in the morning, Mr. Russel." Very crisp. Very businesslike. I had seen her vulnerable and afraid. Now she was back in control of the situation.

She was too decent and too gracious a young woman, though, to feel the need to assert herself further and put me into my place as a lowly dayworker. "Good night then, Cowboy."

"Good night, ma'am."

I packed up a bag of staples and some fence tools and headed out across the grass on the sturdy old grulla. There was a road of sorts, so I followed it. It looked like it hadn't been used much in some years, but in dry country like this the paths beaten by iron-rimmed wheels will last an awful long time. Paths made by hooves too. I had seen many an old buffalo trail and drunk out of more than one buffalo wallow, but the last of the buffs were gone years before I was born. I have never seen a live one.

The country was not empty of game, though. The buffalo might have disappeared in the last century, but little more than a mile from the buildings I began to see pronghorn antelope, a good many of them with little ones at their sides. Most of the bands were small, a half dozen or so at a time, but the bunch must have held between fifty-five and sixty head. Maybe I should have resented them. They were certainly eating grass that properly belonged to Whiskey cows. But heck, the place wasn't over-stocked with beef anyhow. Besides which, I enjoyed looking at them. There were many more here than over toward Kansas, and I found them something of a treat.

I passed close to a low butte that was covered on its shoulders by bare rock and low-growing scrub oak, and a couple mulie does turned their heads enough to stare at me. They certainly weren't either excited or frightened by seeing a horseman. I never did see their fawns, but I suspect they were somewhere near.

The road I was following ran eight or nine miles to the east and continued out of sight across the grass beyond the fence.

Nowadays you see a good many cattle guards at ranch gates, especially on the bigger operations where they can afford automobiles and other niceties, but there was no such here. I got the impression that this gate had been placed before anyone thought in terms of horseless vehicles. It might even have been intended as the main gate at one time for it was wide and sturdily built and a pair of rusted chains showed where a signboard must have hung from the overhead brace timber tying the tall gateposts together.

The gate itself was in bad repair now and the hinges looked solid with rust and dirt. I doubt they had been swung open in years. The wood was solid enough to hold cattle, though, so it was doing all the job it needed to. I left it alone and turned the grulla south.

This particular stretch of fence line would once have been darn expensive to build. It was six strands of a twisted, flat barbed wire that I hadn't seen before and looked sturdy enough to hold up a lot longer than it had so far. At least along here I would not have to worry about the sagging, shoddy things a fellow usually is expected to patch up.

I did find an occasional post that had been broken and needed replacement. The biggest problem there was trying to find a cedar or even a good-sized scrub oak that I could whittle to size with a hatchet. I was beginning to think that if I did much more of this it would pay me to bring a wagon and bucksaw the next time.

It was just as well that I didn't have a wagon, though, for by early afternoon I got into some broken bluffs and gullies where no wagon was likely to travel. Washouts had taken down a good many posts there. They were all intact, but in a few places the posts and wires were in tangles a kid and ball of twine couldn't duplicate, and it took me the rest of the afternoon to get them straightened out and propped up to where they would hold cattle the way they were supposed to. That might have gone a little quicker except a hatchet is a darn poor shovel.

I finished the west-running stretch the next day as far as the railroad tracks and, as I'd been instructed by the Whiskey's boss, turned northeast again toward the headquarters.

I rode into the yard about the middle of the afternoon with thoughts about a long bath and a short rest, but Mrs. Lacey must have been watching for me to come in.

The door of the house burst open and she came rushing out. She was dressed fancier than I had ever seen her except for being barefoot, and she was running for all she was worth.

"Thank goodness you're back, Cowboy. I need you. Ouch!" She began hopping on one foot and favoring the other. "Hurry and change, Cowboy. You have to drive me into town." She paused to catch her breath. "Please. And hurry."

"Yes, ma'am." I booted the grulla toward the horse pen.

CHAPTER 11

Time I got my gear put up and my clothes changed she was outside the bunkhouse door fidgeting and fussing.

"It took you long enough," she snapped as soon as I was back outside.

"Not long enough to bathe, I'm afraid."

She did not look at all sorry that I had missed my bath. "Later," she said. "Right now we need to get on the road, Cowboy, or we'll be too late."

Deliberately I pulled my Bugler pouch out of my pocket and rolled a smoke. "A few minutes one way or the other won't change the way the world turns, ma'am. Learning to take things easy can be a mighty important thing to learn."

"I am entitled to my impatience if I want it, Mr. Russel, and at the moment I want it. If you have any more handy little homilies or cow-country philosophy to deliver to me, please do it while we travel."

"Yes, ma'am. I'll go hitch the team."

"*Team!* My god, Cowboy, I said I'm in a hurry. Crawl out of the nineteenth century and bring me the Dort out of the carriage shed."

"Shall I hitch the team to that then?"

"I . . ."

I stopped her. "Ma'am, I thought I told you but maybe not. I don't know how to drive a car or truck, Miz Lacey."

She looked like she wanted to cuss, but of course she didn't. I gathered there were times when being a lady was a drawback. Patiently, very patiently, she said, "Please bring my case, Cowboy. It is on the table. And you *can* crank an engine, can't you?"

"That much I ought to manage, I guess."

"Fine. I'll drive then. You ride. Quietly."

If she could drive herself, I didn't know why the devil she had to drag me along, but she certainly seemed set on it. I got the case out of the kitchen—it was a portfolio really instead of a travel case like I expected for some reason—and joined her in the carriage shed.

At least she did know how to manipulate the various switches and levers of the heavy sedan. The engine caught on the third spin I gave it, and she coaxed it into a smooth growl. I crawled in on the passenger side and watched her. She was small enough that she had a pillow propped behind her and was sitting on a folded blanket so she could reach the controls and see through the front window, but she seemed proficient enough with the machine. She shuffled the gears and got us moving.

Only after we were away from the ranch and lined out in the ruts at what I thought was an unhealthy speed did she look in my direction again.

"I'm surprised you didn't learn something about driving during the war, Mr. Russel," she commented. It was easy to see that she was trying to make light talk though tension was still pulling the corners of her mouth taut.

She had not intended that to be unkindly and I did not take it so, but still. There it was again. I had thought I was through with that.

"Saddles don't have gears, ma'am, whether there's a war on or not."

"You were in the cavalry then," she said.

As far as I could tell the cavalry was pretty much a dead item since the advent of trenches, bob wire and mustard gas. The one boy I knew who had been kept in a horse cavalry outfit—though most had signed up for that—spent all his time in New Jersey making a brave show on the parade ground. He had been pretty discouraged when he got home. Maybe she had heard something similar about the cavalry.

"I wasn't in the service, ma'am." As far as I was concerned I did not have to explain to her or to anyone else that I had been refused enlistment.

Really, I expected some kind of reaction from her, but she didn't say aye or nay, just kept working to keep the car in the road ruts.

"Do you know anything about repairing flat tires then?" she asked after another half mile or so.

"No, ma'am."

She made a face about that response although she had ignored the other admission of my inadequacy. "This car came with simply unbearable tires," she said. "If I could afford it I would burn these for the pleasure that would give me. Unfortunately, new ones are quite dear these days. Can you at least change wheels? I have two spares on the back."

"I've seen that done. It didn't look too complicated."

She bobbed a rather firmly set chin in a grim nod.

That, at least, explained why she wanted me along. There was a good possibility she would need some manual labor done.

We reached the tracks and bounced across them. The impact of rubber wheels against iron rails was enough to bounce me off the seat and against the roof of the car.

I took my hat off, repaired the squashed crease and replaced it. "Has it occurred to you, ma'am, that your tires might last longer if you didn't use them quite so harshly?"

She nodded quite seriously. "My husband used to tell me that too."

The tires held out somehow past the ranch gate and onto the much better-kept public road. If I thought that would take some of the wear and tear off of them, though, I was mistaken. She merely increased her speed to compensate for the smoother surface. I was quite sure I had never gone so fast, even when riding on passenger trains.

At the fork toward Monument she took a south turn, and within an hour we were on broad, tree-lined city streets. Automobiles were the order of the day here, the only horses I saw being in harness to light delivery vehicles.

Mrs. Lacey knew right where she was going. She parked the auto in front of a three-story-tall brick building and quieted the engine.

"Wait here, Cowboy." She was out and gone before I could get around to open the door and help her down.

I could see an ice cream parlor sign in the next block, but I had no idea how long she would be gone or what she might want next. I pulled my hat forward over my eyes and tried with no success to nap.

She came back after about an hour. She seemed very, very subdued.

"Are you all right, ma'am?"

I helped her into the car but she did not speak and made no motion toward the engine controls. After a minute I walked around the car and climbed into it. "Are you all right?" I asked again.

"Of course, Cowboy. I'm just fine." She certainly did not look or sound all right. "Sorry." She dabbed her knuckles across her eyes and tried to smile. "Would you crank the engine, please?"

"Mrs. Lacey, you have friends in the city. Why don't you spend the night here and we can go back in the morning. We couldn't get back before dark now for sure, and there isn't a thing out there that can't wait until tomorrow."

She smiled, sadly I thought, and shook her head. "Not tonight, I think. Of all times not tonight. I want to be in my own home this evening. Now turn the crank for me, would you please?"

I did as she asked and she drove slowly back the way we had come.

When we were back on the open road in the dying light of day I asked her, "What was this trip all about, ma'am?"

At first she did not say anything but the headlamp light reflecting back through the window showed some shiny tracks down her cheeks.

"This morning," she said, "a boy on a motorcycle came out to tell me my lawyer wanted to see me. As soon as possible, he said.

I thought . . . it might be good news. That was why I was so anxious to get there.

"My lawyer—he used to be Daddy's lawyer too—had been trying to work something out. With the bank. The cattle are mortgaged, of course. Some of them several times over. I told him I would consider mortgaging the land too to clear those debts."

She shook her head with frustration. "Without livestock a ranch can't earn a red cent, and it would take a small fortune to restock the Triple-X if I had to start over from scratch. Except for bulls and the few purebreds Jack bought, we haven't bought an animal, or had to, since my grandfather's time.

"Anyway, as much as I hated the thought of it and as uncertain as it could be with beef prices certain to go down in the next year or two, I thought I had a chance to fight my way out of it. At the very least I thought I had a chance to keep from losing Granddad's ranch." She banged a small fist onto the steering wheel.

"The bank can't—or won't—give me a mortgage now. Some . . . *person*," she made it sound like a cuss word, "is contesting our title to the land now too. On top of everything else, this. The bank can't allow the loan against a clouded title. After all this time, *now* they say the title is clouded."

She was crying hard now, too hard to see I guessed. She pulled the car to the side of the road and stopped while she cried into a handkerchief.

I didn't say anything. There did not seem to be anything I could say. After a while she put the Dort back into gear and drove the rest of the way in silence.

CHAPTER 12

I chased cows and pulled calves a couple days more, but Mrs. Lacey did not say anything to me about more fence repairs and I didn't ask. Dumb brutes are a responsibility you cannot lay aside, but if the fence was going to belong to somebody else he could darn well fix it himself. At least that is the way I would have felt about it, and I was guessing that she did too.

At supper she laid down my six quarters and I pocketed them, trying to pretend that I didn't feel bad about taking them.

"I think I should lay off for a couple more days now, ma'am. The heifers are in good enough shape for a while."

"All right," she agreed listlessly. She had not shown much spirit since that trip in to town, nor could she be blamed for that.

"Is there anything I can bring you?"

She shook her head. Almost as if she expected a negative response she asked, "Will you be coming back?"

"Sure, if you want me to."

She hesitated and bit her underlip before she answered. Her answer was a very brief, very vigorous nod, as if she was giving it in spite of herself.

"Mrs. Lacey, let me tell you something, hear?"

She looked up and waited.

"I've been cowboying here and there wherever a horse could reach for the past ten years or so. I've had some good jobs in my time, and there's been other times when I was 'way down on my luck. I don't have a whole lot to carry with me when I go looking for the next job of work, and I need even less. I've got a little money put by, and I don't need to be adding to it right away. The times I've been down I've ridden the grub line and chopped wood for my groceries. What I'm trying to say is, many and many a time I've done work in swap for a meal and a place to sleep, and I don't find a thing unfair about that. You feed me and let me sleep out in the bunkhouse when I get back, and we'll call it even. I just can't take any more of your money, ma'am. I'll have to quit and move into town if you can't accept my feelings on the subject."

I meant it, too. Those quarters were becoming a torment to me.

The last few days must have taken quite a toll from her pride for she nodded her acceptance of the deal. She wouldn't look at me when she did it, but she agreed.

"Thank you, ma'am. You make me feel a whole lot better." I thought about returning the pay I had gotten recently but decided that would be more insulting than helpful. "Good night, ma'am. I'll be leaving early in the morning so don't look for me at breakfast. I'll see you in a few days."

"Good night, Cowboy."

I was in town by nine the next morning and was feeling primed for a good, solid, cafe breakfast. The place was crowded again, but I passed up a couple empty places while I waited to see where Linda would be waiting the tables. She wasn't in sight when I walked in and hadn't showed up a half hour later, so I gave up on her and decided she must be having a day off. The meal that I got was good enough, but the company was not all I had hoped for.

Afterward I gave my everyday shirt and jeans to a boy whose mother took in washing, and I poked into this shop and that for a little while. I did not really need a thing, but I found a dandy little pocketsize whetstone that I decided I couldn't live without and spent a half hour or so sitting in the sunshine finding out that no matter how cunning it looked it really did not do a very good job. Rather than throw it away, though, I gave it to another kid I saw on the street and figured it was two cents spent that way instead of wasted.

Come two o'clock I went back to the cafe on the assumption

that Linda might be working evenings now, but she still wasn't there. I started to turn away when I noticed Mr. Abelard coming into the place. He recognized me too for he smiled and gave me a handshake.

"Are you just arriving or just leaving, Mr. Russel?"

"Arriving," I told him. "Actually I was looking for Miss Matson, but she doesn't seem to be working today."

"I haven't seen her here for several days," Mr. Abelard said. "Will you join me for dinner?" He smiled. "I could use the company of someone who doesn't care what is in my pockets."

"If I'm quiet during the meal, then, Mr. Abelard, it's because I'm trying to think up some scheme against you."

He threw his head back and got a good laugh out of that. "Somehow I don't think so . . . Cowboy, isn't it? Do you mind?"

"Course not. All my friends call me Cowboy."

"Good. And please call me Curtis. All of my friends do."

This late in the day we had no trouble finding an empty table and the new waitress, obviously no dummy when it came to spotting money, really hopped to get the table wiped clean and a full set of tableware placed for each of us. Mr. Abelard, Curtis, did not seem to notice that the treatment was special. I guess he would be used to it, though.

Dinner was served about the same as breakfast. You had what they offered or you went somewhere else to rustle your meal. We decided to eat.

"I haven't seen you for a few days, Cowboy," Mr. Abelard said while we were waiting.

"No, I've been doing a little work out east of town."

"The same kind your name implies?"

"The very same."

"Do you know this country then?"

I shook my head. "Just got here. Mostly I've worked the Big Empty east and south of here. I sure like this, though."

"Why?" From the way he asked it, that was not a casual question to fill time until the meal was delivered.

So I told him. What I thought about the grass and the water

and what all I had picked up about the climate and the winds and the drift patterns. He kept me talking like that all through dinner and into the coffee afterward.

"Yet you told me you just got here," he said when I wound down some.

"A week, week and a half ago. Something like that."

He shook his head. "I've hired consultants to spend several months investigating a prospect and not give me a report half so lucid as that when they were done," he said. "How do you do it?"

I grinned. "I look a lot and I listen close—don't have a thing against eavesdropping. Besides, I'd like to raise some beef of my own around here. That's what brought me here in the first place. I don't intend to cowboy for somebody else all my life."

He nodded. He could understand that well enough, I believed.

"When I was a youngster," he said, "I started out clerking in a bank. I decided then that I didn't want to spend my life handling someone else's money. I borrowed against my salary to go on the margin against a beef futures deal." He chuckled. "That was the year a big blizzard out here cut the beef supply way down and sent the prices soaring back East. I paid off my loan, quit my job and haven't looked back since."

I did not understand all of that, but the important part of it was clear enough. He knew where I wanted to go because he had made the trip himself.

"Will you be in town awhile now?" he asked.

"Oh, I don't know. Linda, Miss Matson that is, doesn't seem to be around. I might drift on back this evening."

"Let's find out if she'll be back tomorrow then." He lifted a hand in a very small signal and the waitress was right beside us. "We were wondering when Miss Matson would be back to work, young lady."

"Don't know that she will be," the girl said. "The boss said she showed up here the other day with both her eyes moused an' walking all hunched over like she hurt something awful. Took the money she had coming an' took off. Didn't say when she'd be back or if." She glared at both of us a bit suspiciously as if she was wondering if that information might touch a guilty nerve.

I began to get mad myself. Mr. Abelard asked, "Did she say anything about what happened? Or who?"

The girl shook her head. "I never saw her my own self. She talked to the boss."

"Get him." Curtis Abelard was a mild and a pleasant fellow, but there wasn't any doubt about was he issuing an order. When he did, you just knew he was going to be obeyed.

The boss was gotten, but he didn't know a thing more than the girl had told us.

"I have the same thoughts as you about who'd have done it," I said when we were alone again. I guess I was starting to burn pretty good.

"We don't know that."

"I know it well enough. I should've kept on after that night you spoke to me."

He raised his eyebrows so I told him about laying that board across Lonahan. "I should have laid the son-of-a-bitch out for good."

"No, not that," Mr. Abelard said. "There are authorities to take care of this sort of thing, Cowboy."

"They don't do anything until it's already too late for somebody."

"I still say we don't have anything here but suspicions. But I will admit I would like to know more than I do. I may just ask Tyler about it. Or let him tell me without my asking."

"How about now?" I demanded.

"He is usually at William Joyce's place. I think we could go see."

"You bet, Curtis." We paid for our dinners, and Mr. Abelard left a tip that equalled the price of his meal. No wonder he always got good service.

Joyce's place turned out to be the same blind pig where I had seen Curtis before, but neither Tyler nor Lonahan was there at the moment.

"They will be soon enough," Curtis said. "We can wait for them a little while. Would you like a drink while we wait for them?"

Now normally I know enough to leave off that first drink for a fellow cannot get very drunk if he avoids that one, but at that moment I had my dander up and was not thinking much in terms of caution. I decided just one would settle my anger and calm me down maybe.

The bottle they brought to us had a label saying it was twenty-four-year-old stuff which I well believed after I tasted it. It was without doubt the smoothest liquor that ever crossed my tongue, and I was willing to try one more sample when the first was gone. And one more after that.

Pretty soon it tasted even better than before and I began to feel a little warm behind the ears, but I knew quite good and well that whiskey so fine as that was not making me drunk. I knew I was in command of myself. I felt calm and steady and very, very wise.

A man was standing in front of me—I did not remember seeing him arrive there or hearing Curtis Abelard greet him, but they were in the middle of a conversation so they must have spoken without me noticing. The man was Henry Lonahan and I could feel all through me how much I hated that man.

He was standing before my chair and his belt buckle was about at my eye level, and that was where I launched myself.

My firm intention was to claw him down to a proper size and then to kill him.

CHAPTER 13

Well, according to Curtis I didn't do too bad for a fellow giving away maybe four inches and forty pounds and a whole lot of experience. I, personally, do not remember very much about the fight, but I was told that I really had him on the run for about thirty seconds or so there, until he adjusted himself to what was going on and began to take part in it.

I remember throwing a couple real corkers into his bread basket and I remember one good shot to the jaw that would have taken a yearling bull's head clean off his shoulders. Lordy, but that Lonahan was tough.

I remember in a dim kind of way thinking that one more of those would put him down where I could reach him better. I distinctly remember setting myself to throw that just-perfect punch.

I *think* I remember hearing Lonahan laugh and seeing him ball up his right fist.

Next thing I knew I was waking up on a wide old feather bed in a room I had never seen before.

Damnation but no man should ever have to feel that bad. Never.

"It's alive," someone said.

I sat up and wished I could throw up so I would feel better. From the smell of my clothes I guessed that it was too late already. And it hadn't helped a bit.

"I'm not real sure about that." I forced my eyes to pay attention to what was in front of them. It was Curtis. "Did I make a fool of myself?"

He chuckled. "Oh, I wouldn't say that you acquitted yourself too badly. I would not say that you came close to winning, mind, but you did not do too badly everything considered. Would you like some hair of the dog?"

"Lord, no." I would have shook my head, but I was scared of what that might do. "Maybe you didn't notice it, Curtis, but I don't hold my liquor so good. Never have. I kind of get . . . carried away when I've had a few."

"I . . . uh . . . did notice." He looked like he was trying to keep from busting out in a fit of laughter.

"Whupped me, did he?"

"For sure."

I was awake enough now to see what a genuine mess I was, and I apologized to him.

"No problem," he said. He meant it too, by golly. It was plain in his voice. He wasn't upset with me in the slightest. "I did not come straight back with you, by the way." He grinned. "I sent you on ahead. Checking the luggage, as it were. I stayed to have a word with Tyler and Lonahan. *They* thought I was offering an explanation about how you jumped to false conclusions about Mr. Lonahan and a certain Miss Matson. Neither of them turned a hair when I mentioned her. Lonahan, of course, denied any knowledge of the matter. Surprised?"

"No." I sighed. "I guess I did bring it up kind of sudden. Sorry."

"Ah!" He waved his hand and implied that that was the end of that. "Could I ask you a rather personal question, Cowboy?"

He grinned. "Would you happen to have a change of clothing with you?"

"Fortunately for the both of us, I do. A washer lady has them."

"Where?"

"Down near the cafe, across the street from the gasoline pumps."

He nodded. "If you get out of those I will effect an exchange. You'll find a bathrobe and house shoes in the closet. The tub is to the left, the last door."

"Indoor plumbing? That's first class." I shook my head.

And regretted it.

I guess that showed for he grinned again and let himself out the door.

My clothes were too nasty to leave on the bed so I piled them beside the door, got the robe and slippers and went off in search of that tub. I felt a long time overdue for one.

"You won't try anything like that again will you?" Curtis asked over dinner. It was already too late for breakfast when we got to the cafe, even though the last I really remembered well was the previous afternoon.

"No, I reckon not. Not straight out and to his face anyhow. I'm not so proud that I'm stupid."

"Good. Because we are about to have company."

Darned if he wasn't right too. Tyler and his shadow joined us just like we were all good friends. Tyler shook my hand hello and called me by name. Lonahan gave me a cold, superior sort of look that did not do a whole lot toward making me start to like him.

"I understand you were laboring under a misplaced assumption yesterday, Mr. Russel," Tyler said.

"What I was laboring under," I said, "was a load of too much booze. I sure am sorry about that." That was the natural truth too. If I'd been sober I would have had sense enough to find another two-by-four and not to quit until Lonahan's head was scrambled. So I truly was sorry about what I had done.

"Your apology is accepted I'm sure," Tyler said brightly. He gave Lonahan a pointed look.

Lonahan in turn grunted once to show that he was indeed accepting my apology. Darn decent of him, I thought.

"Well, that seems to be settled," Curtis said cheerfully. When I looked at him he gave me a quick flicker of a wink. He wasn't buying these fellows any more than I was.

Tyler and Lonahan ordered their meals. Curtis and I were just finishing ours.

"I'm glad we found you here, Curtis," Tyler said. "I was . . .

uh . . . wanting to talk to you yesterday. It didn't seem the time for it." He laughed. Maybe it was just my interpretation, but the laugh sounded phony to me. "I got word from my man in Denver yesterday." He smirked. "A little advance knowledge never hurts anyone, and I'm willing to share, Curtis. I'd still like to reach an agreement with you, you know."

"I know, Mel. We already discussed that."

If Mr. Abelard was panting to learn what Tyler's advance word was, he certainly managed to hide it well. Since he did not ask, Tyler told him anyway.

"Your information about the land values is no longer valid, Curtis. A claimant has filed suit for title to a large share of the property. Unclear title; no collateral for loan financing. As simple as that. It shouldn't be made public for a few days yet. I thought you would want to know."

Mr. Abelard nodded. "I appreciate that, Mel."

"I . . . uh . . . happen to know that this title claimant could be induced to sign over his interest in the property, Curtis. He would sign a quit-claim deed in our favor. Since the matter is still unsettled, I imagine we could secure that for a nominal amount. Equal shares, I would suggest."

Mr. Abelard seemed to be deep in thought. He gave Tyler a very tight smile. "Let me get back to you about that, Mel."

"Of course, Curtis. I know you'll want to verify what I say. If you have a contact . . . but who am I to advise you? Of course you will know where to go and how to get it. They will give you the claimant's name, of course. I can give you the claimant."

Mr. Abelard's smile never changed. He shook Tyler's hand and thanked him again and we left.

"Mr. Tyler seems a bit greedy," Abelard said when we were on the street.

"I don't understand. I mean, I understand about the clouded title and all that. I can see how that insures the failure of the Whiskey and that as quit-claim in your favor would give you a leg up on the auction. Any other buyer would still have to clear the title. You'd already be clear. But I think I'm missing something about it."

"Damn well less than I would have expected of a wandering cowboy, Cowboy. You do manage to surprise me at times. And the reason I say Tyler is a greedier than normal human being is because he is trying to run a confidence game on me at the same time as he maneuvers me into a partnership agreement."

"Okay, now I'm confused for fair."

"It's simple enough. The title claim is false, of course. It couldn't possibly hold up in the long run, but a title suit can be a very long run indeed. The Three-X hasn't anything like that amount of time left before a bankruptcy declaration.

"Since our friend Tyler is the one who can find the claimant, we can safely assume that Tyler arranged for the claim to be filed. That would be simple enough to do. Check early records for the name of a close neighbor. Have someone assume the name and pretend a direct descendency. Concoct a cross-claim story, possibly under preemption laws, *those* records are horribly maintained and the surveys are often unbelievably crude and unreliable. File the suit, and then of course the holder of the claimant's quit-claim is in the driver's seat. How did you put it? He has a 'leg up' on all the other auction bidders. Since they know it, they don't bid. The sale goes through at the minimum needed to satisfy the liens, and the new owners do quite well, thank you." He snorted.

"Tyler doesn't seem content, though, to get half the Three-X ranch for virtually nothing. He wants me to pay off his Tyler-made—I do hope you don't mind a bit of a pun there—claimant and provide him with some cash at the same time.

"A suitable claimant could be found for a few hundred dollars. Less if you don't care about the quality or appearance of the man you are bribing. Call it that much again for the lawyer who would handle your shady deal. Call it a maximum investment of five hundred.

"You can be sure, though, if I were to agree to this partnership it would cost us, say, ten thousand equally divided between the two of us. You can be just as sure that Tyler would take the money to the claimant. Or so he would say. What he would do would be to pocket my money as extra profit. The claimant is already his, bought and paid for going into the deal. Very crude of him, really."

"How can you be so sure about it?"

"Oh, a couple things. One, when he started talking to me about an agreement, he was hoping for a quarter of the deal. With his homemade leverage he's upped it to half now. Two, all of this comes suspiciously close behind a comment I had made to him suggesting that a good manager or a determined one could salvage the Three-X with the help of a good banker and a good lawyer. The banker could provide mortgage money for operating capital while the lawyer fought a delaying action on the original liens. Marvelous fellows at procrastination, lawyers." He shrugged. "I make that suggestion, he removes the possibility. Simple."

Curtis laughed. "A third reason I can't accept Tyler's scheme is that I've had a great deal of experience with confidence men in my time. I daresay I have met some experts in the field. *Much* better at it than Mel Tyler."

"In that past experience, how did you come out?" I couldn't help asking it.

"Oh, sometimes I ignored them. Frequently, I've found a way to turn a profit from them. I rather enjoy that when it happens."

After listening to the pleasure in his voice when he said that, I decided it might be the Christian, charitable thing to do to feel sorry for any confidence man who tried to pull his game on Curtis Abelard. This old boy was not exactly your basic dummy.

I was also beginning to feel like all of a sudden I had gone back to school in a new and higher field of education. There are certain things that you just don't learn about while cowboying. Hadn't ever much wanted to learn about those things either.

We walked on back to Mr. Abelard's rented house.

CHAPTER 14

The damned, stupid bay horse had a terrible time finding his way back to the Whiskey, possibly because I myself had had no trouble finding the whiskey.

I left Mr. Abelard in town in the late afternoon with the idea that I had had just about all of Monument that I could enjoy at the moment. I mean, it was a nice town and all that, but big money tends to make people sneaky and to attract some nasty ones, and I really prefer for things to be straight-forward and clean.

Anyway, I said my good-byes and got my horse and happened to be passing the blind pig on my way out and happened to get to thinking how rough I felt and how good that stuff of Curtis Abelard's had tasted the day before. Which is a problem I sometimes have once I get started and one of the reasons why I really don't like to get started in the first place.

The point is, I laid in some traveling supplies in the form of a quart Mason jar that tasted better with each successive swallow, and so I got a little lost and spent the night cuddled up to a tuft of friendly grass until about 3 A.M. when I woke up cold and stiff but awake enough to make it the rest of the way back to the bunkhouse.

Since I was that far awake anyhow I doused my head in some water and went in search of breakfast. I would trust my face to a razor blade some other time.

It was time for breakfast and past time, but the house was dark and empty looking. Any other time I would have done the decent thing since the lady was not expecting me back any particular time and I would have gone back to the bunkhouse to see if I could find something in my gear and let the lady sleep. That was any normal time. Now I was cranky and hung over and I damn well wanted some hot coffee and a platter full of greasy chow, and I wanted it now.

I barged on into the kitchen, stumbled over the chairs a couple times and eventually found a wall lamp. There were dirty dishes on the table so I cleared them away and piled them in the sink.

I had not exactly been quiet about doing any of this. The truth is that I was hoping Mrs. Lacey would wake up and, after I apologized suitably for disturbing her, would offer to cook my breakfast.

She didn't show, so after a couple impatient minutes I resigned myself to doing it without her.

The range firebox had not been cleaned out recently but I did not feel like doing the job now, even though the ash was cold and dead and it would have been a good time for a thorough cleaning. I never gave a thought to how dead that ash was.

There was dried grass and a kindling in a box beside the stove and coal in a hopper nearby. A couple minutes and a more than adequate application of kindling was all it took to get the coal burning. Once it was going I stuffed the box with all it would burn and clanged the iron door shut. Still no Mrs. Lacey. She seemed to be a pretty good sleeper.

While the range was coming to heat I drew a pot of water and while I was at it filled the hot water reservoir in the stove. That hadn't been done in a while either.

I found the coffee and dumped some into the pot and belatedly remembered that I had intended to bring some goodies back with me from town. I hadn't done it and could not at the moment remember if I had bought the stuff and not brought it or if I hadn't bought it to start with.

The pantry was a big, cold room off the kitchen with a lot more shelves than food in it right now. There was still beef hanging from when I had butchered, so I sliced off a hunk of that and carried out some flour and lard and a tin of baking powder as well for biscuit-making, which I don't do very well but can at least manage passably.

By the time the biscuits were put together and in the oven and the meat was sliced and on the stove, the coffee was at a good boil and should have reached a drinkable color.

Mrs. Lacey still hadn't shown up although by now it was full daylight and I had been making noises in her kitchen for half an hour.

It came into my head to carry a cup of coffee to her. That was not entirely a thoughtful and generous thing for me to do. By now I was feeling somewhat sorry for myself and wanted some sympathy for having to make my own breakfast before a hard day's work. Poor me. I was almost ready to break down in tears on my own behalf.

I found a mug, couldn't remember if she took milk or sugar but decided she could drink it black this time even if she did.

I had never been in any part of the house except the kitchen, but there was good light now and I figured I could find my way around in someone else's home just fine. I armed myself with a steaming mug of black coffee and went off to let her know how badly I was being used around here.

The door out of the kitchen let into a sort of hallway beside a staircase and to a sort of entryway or foyer beyond that. It was a pretty swell looking place from what I could see. Fancy rugs and polished wood and lamps with hand-painted globes. There were doors to left and right and the staircase leading up to the rear. I took the stairs and didn't worry about the treads creaking.

Upstairs there were four doors, all of them closed, and darn little light reaching the landing. All four of them opened onto bedrooms, one quite large and the other three pretty small. Only one, one of the smaller ones, showed any sign of recent use, and it was empty too at the moment, the bed carefully made and a pretty throw pillow laid out on top of the sham-covered pillows. No sign of Mrs. Lacey though I opened her wardrobe and looked into it to see if she might have heard me coming and be hiding. To think why she might bother to hide from me was beyond my reasoning at the moment. I looked anyway. The wardrobe was crammed near to bursting with fancy looking dresses, but I didn't find Mrs. Lacey there.

While I was at it I inspected the other empty rooms too. There wasn't much of anything at all in the two small ones, just furniture and bedding and empty basins and pitchers on their washstands. The big room had the usual furniture and two wardrobes. One of those held woman's clothes, which I guessed was the overflow from Mrs. Lacey's room. The other had a man's clothing in it. They were mostly suits and flannel blazers and such natty gear as that with only one nearly new pair of jeans and one decently serviceable heavy coat among them. I took that collection to be Jack Lacey's stuff.

Still no lady of the house, though.

By now I had decided that she'd gone off visiting someone and hadn't thought to leave me a note, but also by now I'd become what you might call nabby if not downright nosy. I took a swallow of the coffee I had intended for her and decided if I was going to do it at all, I might as well get full satisfaction from it. I would investigate the downstairs too and by golly the cellar if there was one.

On one side of the house downstairs was a living room and kind of a library with a big old table in the middle of it that looked like it might once have been intended for eating use. I nosed through both rooms and admired the books and wondered how I could ask for the loan of some of them without her knowing I'd been prowling around. I guess I was starting to come more to my own mind than that corn juice had made me.

I thought about not going through the last door, which was on the same side of the house as the kitchen and forward of it, but there was only the one left and I decided to make it a clean sweep. It's a good thing I did.

The last room was a study or den or office, whichever a body might want to call it. There was a couch facing away from the door toward a small, stone fireplace and on the other end of the room a handsome desk outfit with several wood chairs beside it and a bunch of ledgers piled atop of it. Between those two ends the wall had on it a rack of rifles and several game heads including an awfully nice bighorn ram. I almost envied whoever had taken that old boy although I am not much given to envy as a normal course of things.

The rifles weren't of much account, a Krag and a modern sporter with a bolt action and a couple Winchesters, one a '95 and the other I think an '86. Down over the fireplace, though, there was hanging an old-timey long gun that looked from where I was standing like it had a flint lock. It looked in good shape too, and as I was curious about it I ambled down that way.

I never got that far.

When I came level with the leather couch I saw there was a body stretched out on it.

CHAPTER 15

Lord God, it was Mrs. Lacey.

I dropped down beside her and peered at her close. I was hoping she was just asleep, in spite of all the noise I'd been making, but it wasn't that at all. I couldn't see her breathing.

She was stretched out on her back like she was laid out for burying. She was fully dressed in a going-to-town-quality garment and her feet were crossed at the ankles. Her hands were resting on her stomach with the fingers laced together. Her hair was done up neat and tidy with pins to hold it in place. It was too short for a bun but it looked like she had spent some time on it to make it nice.

It was her face that got to me the most. Every time I had seen her before she had looked nice but not exceptionally so. Now she looked quite pretty. I realized that this was probably the first time I had ever seen her face when she was not under tension. In repose she was really a very attractive young woman.

There were certainly no marks on her or signs that anyone had done her harm. From the way she was lying there I believed she did it herself and expected, even wanted, to die. It seemed an awful waste.

I reached out a hand to touch her forehead. I suppose that was a way of saying good-bye and I'm sorry. Her skin was warm to the touch.

I had expected her to be cold, and I was surprised by what I found. And of a sudden hopeful.

There was no mirror handy that I could use to test for breath, but I bent close over her. I wasn't exactly sure but I thought I could feel a small passage of air. I wet my fingertips and held them near, but I still wasn't sure. If she was still breathing it was mighty little. There was a way to be sure.

The neck of her dress reached high on her throat. I peeled the cloth back and laid my fingers on the delicate hollow at her throat. There just beneath the skin I could feel a faint but determined flutter of her pulse. She was still alive. Maybe not by much, but she wasn't gone yet.

I scooped an arm under her shoulders and raised her to a sitting position. My first thought was to pour some coffee into her, and I had been carrying that cup of it when I walked into the room. The cup wasn't in my hand any longer and I had absolutely no idea what I might have done with it. I might have slung it out the window when I first saw her for all I could remember now.

I absolutely was not going to leave her here while I went to fetch more, though. I knew that for a fact. I slipped my other arm under her knees and carried her with me to the kitchen.

She lay propped in a chair like a rag doll with too little stuffing while I got a cup and splashed some hot coffee into it. If it burned her that would be regrettable, but she could live with that annoyance. I hoped. I pulled her jaw open and began to pour. Most of the stuff ran back out of her mouth but after a moment she moved just the least bit and I saw her throat contract in a swallow.

"That's it. *That's* it! Swallow." I poured again and more after that. By the third or fourth time she was swallowing all I gave her. "Keep it up."

I got more coffee.

There was smoke seeping out around the oven door. I remembered putting a pan of biscuits in there. The hell with them, they could wait until later. The skillet of meat must have been sitting on a fairly cool part of the range top for it wasn't yet burning. I set it off the stove to the work counter while I was there at the coffee pot.

She took another half cup of the stuff, and I didn't stop with it until she sputtered and coughed and shook her head.

"Hot," she protested in a very weak voice. But she had spoken. She had come that far up from wherever she had been. I gave a little yelp of joy and encouragement.

"Right. Too hot. That's fine," I told her. "That's just fine." I set the cup aside and dragged her to her feet. I didn't know what she had done to get herself this way, but I had the idea that if I treated her like I would a drunk it might do some good. It hadn't hurt so far. I began to walk her up and down the length of that kitchen.

I was not in the best of shape to start with, and of course she was even worse. Between us we made a pretty rough pair, but what we lacked in coordination we more than made up for in sheer stamina. Once we got started we just kept going until at the end there I was practically dragging that poor lady by the hair to keep her moving. When she commenced to fuss about the treatment I was giving her, I took it as a good sign and felt encouraged to do more. By the time we ran out of coffee and my feet were several days' worth sore, she was acting almost human.

I sat her down at the table and said, "Ma'am, you did a very stupid thing, you know."

If she knew that, she was not admitting it yet. She asked for some more coffee. She had already drunk enough of that stuff to refloat the *Maine,* yet she wanted more. "Yes, ma'am," I told her.

The fire in the stove had gone out, the coffeepot was empty and the breakfast I had started to fix those hours earlier was hours ruined. I started the whole process over again.

When the meal was ready I didn't ask her if she wanted any. I gave it to her and was prepared to get my back up if she argued over eating it. She didn't.

I watched her put down every bite though she acted like she was forcing it there toward the end. When she was done I asked, "Why did you do a thing like that, ma'am?"

The look she gave me I read as disgust. "That is a rather dumb question, Cowboy."

"I don't think so. A person your age has more to live for than past pride, you know. There's always hope for the future. Hope for revenge if nothing else. Did you ever think of that, Mrs. Lacey? Even if the very worst things possible really come to pass, you can still look forward to finding that husband of yours." I looked her close in the eye and asked, "What would you do if you saw him on the street tomorrow, ma'am? What would you do if he showed up at the door tomorrow thinking he had a scheme to make more off of you?"

Now what I was doing was not exactly an idea that was mine alone. Some of the boys back from the Great War spoke of cases that they called shell shock. Which was nothing new. I remembered hearing gray-bearded old vets from the War for Southern Independence talk about fellows freezing on the line. I'd got the impression that what happened was not so much fear as a lack of hope, and Mrs. Lacey certainly was lacking hope.

The old-timers had talked about kicking their buddies to get their minds back on what was going on around them. Knocking them around themselves or the officers whacking them with the flats of their swords.

That kind of treatment did not exactly seem appropriate here, but some of the fellows that recently were doughboys instead of cowboys told me a man would sometimes come out of his funk if he was given something to look forward to. Getting back at Fritz or getting a pass to go find Fifi—either one of those might work, they said, so long as the fellow with the shell shock had something he could hope toward.

Well, in this case it would have been pretty darn indelicate to get into the one side of that, but I figured Mrs. Lacey should have all the reason in the world to want to get back at Jack Lacey. It sure seemed worth the try.

She took my question serious, too. She didn't throw out any flip answer but gave it some thought before she responded.

"I think," she said slowly, "I think I would not want to kill him. Not right away." Her voice got a dreamy, far-away kind of quality to it. "I think it would be nice if someone were to truss him up for me, so he could not get loose or run away. And I

think that if I could just be left alone with him for a while . . .
yes, I think that would be very nice, Cowboy. Very nice indeed."

The way she said that and the look in her eyes when she did,
well, I hoped if it ever happened I would not have to see the re-
sults of it afterward. I've heard a lot of yarns about squaws mess-
ing with Indians' captives. Now I understood better why that was
regarded as so awful.

"I'll clean up these dishes now, ma'am, and then you and me—
you and I, I mean—are going for a little walk or maybe a canter
around the place."

"That shouldn't be necessary, I . . ."

"Please. Humor me, Miz Lacey. I'll feel better seeing you out
in the fresh air where I can keep an eye on you."

"I'm tired now. Too tired for that."

"I'll hitch up the buggy. The drive will do you good."

She gave up then. Her attention seemed to be elsewhere anyway, and I was betting it was on Jack Lacey and a closed room
with just the two of them in it. I decided I had done all right with
that idea of mine. Hate like that can be fine fuel for a body's will-
power. I began clearing the dishes into the sink for washing.

CHAPTER 16

Once it was over and done with it seemed to be really over and done with. I mean, she did not try to hide from it or pretend that it had not happened. She spoke of it freely over the next couple days. I don't think she would have done that if her mood was such that she might be thinking of trying it again. At least that was my judgment of the matter, although I am certainly no authority on why people do the things they do.

Still, I felt more comfortable knowing where she was and what she was doing, so I asked her to come along in the buggy while I worked the heifer pasture again. She did so with an air of amusement as if she was humoring me by going along, and I took that as a good sign too.

What she had done was taken some leftover bits of this and that in the medicine chest, all the things that were or sounded like they might be opiates. Fortunately for her they had not added up to enough of the stuff to do any lasting damage.

Her attitude seemed good, and several times she mentioned Jack Lacey and a few things she would like to do to him or have done to him. I gathered that she was still giving that some thought.

I was doing some thinking myself. About people like Jack Lacey who would bleed this lady dry of all her family had ever built. About people like Mel Tyler who would stack the deck against her so they could scavenge what was left and toss the bones aside once Lacey was finished. I thought, too, about my own dreams for owning a piece of this land.

I wanted some of it. I couldn't ever say that I did not. But it was equally true that whatever I eventually got I wanted to be able to take pride in. I didn't want to ever have to think of myself as a bone-picker or be ranked with the likes of Tyler and Lonahan.

So I listened while the lady talked and I did my thinking until I was able to be peaceable in my own mind, and after a couple days of pondering it I stayed at the table after supper and asked could we have a talk.

"Of course, Cowboy. If I didn't trust you by now, after all the help you've given me, there would be something awfully wrong with me."

"Good, ma'am. I appreciate that." I guess I coughed a little bit. "I suppose I should tell you to start with that I came over to this country after I heard the Whiskey was in trouble. I had it in mind—and still do, Miz Lacey—to see if I could get part of this land if it is sold on the cheap. The thing is, I couldn't do that with a clear conscience if I took advantage of you or didn't do everything I can to help you find a way out. Can you understand what I'm saying?"

She nodded. "My grandfather would have understood that too, I believe. He had a *very* old-fashioned sense of honor."

"Yes, ma'am. Well, what I've been thinking is this. I know about those claims against the title to your granddaddy's land. I know those clouds are just false as false could be, too. No way to prove it, of course, but that's the thing that's really put your back to the wall. Without that you could raise enough money on mortgage notes to pull yourself back above water, right?"

"I think so, yes."

"Uh-huh. But have you thought too, ma'am, that if you had enough money to meet the first and the worst of the claims against your livestock, you could hold out long enough that those land claims would die of their own weight. I mean, the man that invented those claims just naturally *knows* that he can't prove them at law. Not when he made them up out of whole cloth, he can't. So it doesn't stand to reason that he will pour money down the rat hole by taking in a lawyer to raise. Once you show him a long fight, he is out of it. The man's crooked, but he isn't stupid."

She shrugged. "I hadn't thought of that—had no reason to—but I can agree that it would work that way, certainly, *if* I had the cash to free my breeding stock and operate until I have a calf crop to sell. As it happens, though, I have nowhere near that amount of money. Or any amount of money, really."

"Just bear with me a little longer if you would please, ma'am. Now I've been doing some listening around here for a couple days, an' some calculating.

"Yesterday you told me your mister took out three-year notes on something like six thousand head of mixed stock. About a hundred fifty thousand worth, which means if you can come up with fifty thousand this year, they don't have any choice but to carry you on to the next year's payment time, right?"

"Of course. But I don't have fifty thousand dollars. I don't have six thousand animals either. Jack sold the steers. I probably have, oh, four thousand, maybe forty-five hundred left. And that would include the new calves. They don't count for anything."

"No, but they would next year. The last quote I saw, feeders were going a little over seven dollars a hundred pounds."

She nodded. "Seven twenty-six when I was in town. That doesn't help me a bit this year."

"Just . . . stay with me here. We're agreed so far.

"Now, this morning you were saying that the claims against the Whiskey land cover *almost* all of it. I'd heard that in town too, but never paid it much mind, you see. That's important, I think. This morning you said your granddaddy's original homestead and preemption filings couldn't be touched. That should be a couple thousand acres maybe?"

She thought about it. "A little more than that, I think. I know both my grandparents filed, and one son and a couple hands. That was the way they did things then, you know."

I gave her the nod.

"If I remember correctly there is about thirty-eight hundred acres still unclouded." She snorted. "I might be able to squeeze a hundred cows onto that little patch of ground. If I had a hundred cows that were not encumbered."

"Yes, ma'am, but if your granddaddy was like all the old cow-men I've known, that little patch is the headquarters ground. Has the best water, the best hay-cutting bottoms, generally would be the most valuable piece of the Whiskey."

"It would be, of course."

"Ma'am, that patch of good ground is still clear enough to mortgage, you know."

She sighed. "Cowboy, I appreciate what you are trying to do. I really do. It is very kind of you, very thoughtful indeed. But I am afraid, well, I don't mean to make light of you at all, but I couldn't *begin* to raise fifty thousand dollars against thirty-eight hundred acres no matter how fine it was. Land just isn't that val-uable. I'm sorry. But I do thank you for trying to help."

I grinned at her. "Ma'am, I do wish you would let this old cowboy finish."

She gave me a tolerant smile and nodded. "Of course."

Well, she was welcome to think she was humoring me. Just so long as she was listening to me.

"I told you already, ma'am, it's my hope to buy land of my own someday. I'm not ignorant of land prices. Around here I see it advertised as low as eight dollars the acre and as high as four-teen, most of it in the ten- to twelve-dollar range."

She nodded. She might as well have. I knew I was right.

"The way people are thinking about the Whiskey right now you won't get any loans of three-quarters of the value. You *might* get half on a low value or a third of a higher one. Let's say you can get a loan at four dollars the acre. Ma'am, that is a bit more than fifteen thousand dollars you would have in your pocket then. Or your handbag as the case may be."

"A far cry from fifty thousand," she said.

"Maybe not as far as you think. You already agreed that feeders are bringing at least seven and a quarter per hundred. Light feeders, even after they dock you for shrinkage and dock you for being lightweights and dock you for all the other little things they can find to carp about, still a five-hundred-pound feeder calf is going to be worth something over thirty dollars, Mrs. Lacey."

"And if I had a thousand of them I could manage, I agree," she said. "But I don't have them."

"Ma'am, down in Old Mexico it is possible to buy a five-hundred-pound feeder for ten Yankee dollars. Maybe less if you make the right connection an' find an old boy who's hungry for a commission."

It gave her a start, I could see. It also gave her pause. I was willing to bet she was toting up the possibilities. I knew what she would come up with. It could work out slim but possible. Very definitely possible.

She thought about it and thought about it, and eventually she came up to the question I'd known she would have to think about if she was at all bright enough to justify her bloodlines and operate a place as big as the Whiskey.

"Cowboy, if it is that simple to treble your money, why isn't everyone doing it?"

"Ma'am, there is a very simple answer to that. Two of them, really. One is that Mexico is not a real safe place to be right now. The area where I'm talking about, ole Villa is still down there playing general and sometimes shooting at people."

"And the other?"

I grinned at her. "Ma'am, this little deal that I am proposing, it ain't entirely legal."

CHAPTER 17

She drove us into town again the next morning, and I discovered that a sense of urgency was not the only thing that made her push the big Dort to the limits of safety and good sense. Apparently she was just plain a fast driver. At least when she got in near town she slowed down. She said she couldn't afford any speeding tickets.

She parked at the bank, and this time there wasn't any waiting in the car while she conducted her business. I was invited inside right along with her.

The place was very, very dignified. Polished wood and gleaming brass and hushed voices. The old gentleman whose office we went to was a good match for the place. He wore a batwing collar that looked like it would have survived a steam bath unwilted; it wouldn't have dared to droop and ruffle his dignity. He had pince-nez glasses that he wore with an air that made me think of a monocle instead of glasses, and his high-button shoes looked like something out of the past century. He would have been perfect for the part if they had put him in one of those moving pictures and had him play an old-fashioned banker. I got the impression he was one of those people who would call his wife "missus" even in private. Mrs. Lacey made the introductions, and from the way he treated her in the conversation that followed you would have thought she was his biggest depositor. Very formal, very respectful.

She explained what she wanted and had me explain how I figured to use it to help her.

The banker steepled his fingers and looked stern and explained in some detail how he could not recommend any course of action that would be so risky, and that he *certainly* would not countenance anything that would be outside the law.

He cleared his throat and smiled a tight, thin-lipped little smile. There was also, he said, his obligation to the stockholders of the bank. A note against the Triple-X would be good business, whether it was repaid or went into default. And it *did* seem her only possibility for survival, however slim the likelihood of success.

He could, he said, approve a loan based on a rate of $4.25 per acre against an assumed value of $8.50 per acre, repayable at 4 percent interest over a period of ten years. That would give her an operating capital now of . . . he stopped to calculate the amount . . . $16,150 cash, less a $10 documentary and filing fee for services. He was smiling that tight, thin smile again.

Mrs. Lacey was ready to accept and have him draw up the papers, I was sure, but I butted in and said, "The lady could take a day or two to think over your offer, couldn't she, sir? I mean, this is a pretty big step and an even bigger gamble. She maybe should think about it overnight first."

"I quite agree with you, young man. And, of course, there is no hurry about the acceptance. You may consider the offer firm, Mrs. Lacey. Take as long as you like to make up your mind."

There was a certain amount of polite talk required to end the conversation and then some handshaking and finally an invitation for me to stop in and visit with him any time I might have banking requirements. Now *that* was a sign of old school politeness for he would have had me pegged as a plain old cowhand from the moment I first showed up in his doorway.

Once we got back out onto the sidewalk, boy did I get an odd look.

"What in the *world* was that about, Cowboy? I thought that was exactly what we came here for. Then you jump in and want me to wait. I don't understand that at all. Why, even the amount was about what we expected."

"Yes, ma'am, I know, but I happened to think while we were in there, you see. The bank was willing to go for that amount and if they would today they would go the same amount next week. Well, I had this idea. You know you can get that much. It won't hurt to shop around a bit and see if you can get more. If you can, great. If not, you have the sixteen thousand in the bag. I figured it wouldn't hurt to do the shopping before you make it final."

"I see, but really, Cowboy, I wouldn't know where else to look for a mortgage loan. Why, my family has always done business with this bank. No one else would know a thing about me or about the ranch. I just wouldn't know where else to turn."

"Yes'm, but . . . uh . . . I might have some thoughts on that too, you see."

She smiled. "I might have guessed as much. Tell me about it."

So I did. When I was done she said, "I suppose it can't hurt to try, can it? Would you like me to drive you to Monument now? It would practically be on our way going home."

"Thank you, ma'am, but if you don't mind I think I would rather go in by myself."

"If you prefer."

She drove us back, her speed hindered by one flat tire that I fixed. Actually, considering the bucking-horse quality of her driving, it was a wonder she didn't have more tire troubles than she did. It sure spoke well of the toughness of rubber.

We were back at the Whiskey in time for a late lunch, after being all the way into town, conducting that business at the bank and coming all the way back again. Much as I disliked the machines, I guess, in truth, that had quite a lot to say about the speed and reliability of the modern automobile. If it is speed you want, you just can't beat a machine, soulless and unfeeling things though they are.

After lunch I saddled my horse and headed for Monument.

Curtis Abelard was at his home, and I was glad to find him there. I wanted our discussion to be as private as possible.

"Cowboy! What a delightful surprise. Come in. No, not empty-handed. Bring your baggage inside. I have too much extra space here for you to be hiring a room. Go get your things now and put your horse into the shed around back. I'll tell the cook we have a guest at supper. Go on now."

He disappeared inside the house before I could even thank him.

It would have served no purpose to argue with his generosity, and anyway I enjoyed the man's company. I moved my things inside and over a pre-dinner cup of coffee—he had offered a snort of that excellent whiskey, but I wasn't taking any chances of going overboard this time—I made my confession.

"Mr. Abelard, I came into town this time for the purpose of discussing some business with you."

"A proposition, Cowboy?" He smiled. "Since it comes from you, I am willing to listen." He laughed outright. "But I warn you, since I arrived here I've heard just about every scheme imaginable."

"Our good friend, Mr. Tyler?" I asked, laughing along with him.

"Oh yes. Tyler and others even less subtle, if you can imagine that. Now. What is your idea, Cowboy?"

I told him what I had in mind, and I told him too that Mrs. Lacey had a loan offer from the bank. I did not tell him how much that offer was.

"Mmm. Rather interesting." I certainly did not have to draw any pictures for Curtis. He was quite bright enough to figure the possibilities for himself. "This mortgage would be against the heart of the Three-X, which would give me a tremendous advantage against the other hundred thousand or so acres in the event of a default. And if there is to be no default, I've been wasting my time here waiting for one. This at least would give me a small profit from interest on the investment. If the bank were to hold the mortgage, of course, they would assume control upon default. And they would certainly hold the keystone property for sale at full market value, regardless of bankruptcy proceedings that might involve the lower value acreage. Do you agree, Cowboy?"

"Yes, sir, I do. I see it that way exactly. Holding the note would give you an advantage over everyone else. On the other hand, it would also be giving Mrs. Lacey her one shot at avoiding bankruptcy."

"An opportunity she will have by way of the bank if not through me, though."

"That's true too. She'll have a chance, one way or the other."

"Then really there is only one sensible choice open to me. Of course I will make her the loan. What terms do you suggest, Cowboy?"

I shook my head. "I couldn't advise you about that, Curtis. I'm working for the lady, you know. And I happen to like you as a friend, if you don't mind me saying so. Since I know what the bank will loan," I shrugged, "I just don't think it would be right for me to make any suggestions. I really don't."

"Well spoken, Cowboy. I fully agree. Do . . . uh . . . do you mind if I ask you a blunt question?"

"Try me. If I object, I won't answer."

"Fair enough." He cleared his throat. "What I was wondering was, since you hope to benefit from a bankruptcy too . . . ?"

I couldn't help but chuckle. "Ah yes. Why am I trying to help Mrs. Lacey make money this way? A couple reasons. One is so I can look myself in the face when I shave. The other, well, with enough of a herd slipping out of Mexico to make the effort worthwhile anyhow, the truth is that I figure to carry some of my own savings along and kind of ride along on her coattails. She'll be providing the *vaqueros* and travel expenses and what-not. I intend to buy a few steers of my own to turn the same kind of profit." I grinned. "I hope."

"I certainly cannot fault a man for trying to turn a profit, Cowboy. But why haven't you done it on your own already?"

"Curtis, I am not a very wealthy man. With the little bit I can afford to gamble, by the time I paid expenses there wouldn't be anything left to buy cattle with. I need those coattails, Curtis."

He nodded. "I'll want some time to consider my loan offer. You said thirty-eight hundred acres?"

"Yes."

"I'll let you know after dinner."

I was sure he already knew land values around here a lot better than I did. What he would be doing now would be trying to second-guess the bank's mortgage offer and then top it. But just barely. It was an interesting problem he faced and one I could not help him with if I wanted to keep his respect. Which I did.

"In that case, sir, I'll leave you to your figuring. If you don't mind, I'll borrow something from your library and read until suppertime."

"Of course, Cowboy. And before I forget . . . thanks."

"*Por nada*. Maybe it will work out for all of us."

"I'll see you at dinner then, Cowboy." He was already deep in thought.

CHAPTER 18

I was grinning when I got back to the Whiskey late that next morning.

It didn't take Mrs. Lacey long to catch my mood. "What did he say? Tell me. Please!"

My grin got all the wider. "I told him to go ahead and get the papers drawn. He's doing that today, ma'am. I told him we could come in to sign them tomorrow morning."

"But what did he *say*? How much did he offer? Is it *that* much better than the bank?"

I laughed outright. I couldn't help it. "The bank offered you four and a quarter per acre, right?"

She nodded.

"Well my friend Mr. Abelard will loan you . . . are you ready? . . . five seventy-five an acre."

She squealed and clapped her hands. "Oh, Cowboy. Oh, how marvelous. How utterly, totally marvelous. Oh my *Lord!* What does that come to? You did figure it up, didn't you?"

"Oh, we figured it all right. Let me check to make sure I'm right now." I dipped two fingers into my vest pocket for the slip of paper I had used to copy Mr. Abelard's figures on. "It comes to"—I grinned and held her in suspense a moment longer—"exactly $21,850. Ma'am, you can buy a good many *corriente* steers for that. For a fact you can."

"Oh, *Cowboy!*" She whirled herself around and around the kitchen floor and eventually dropped into one of the chairs. She looked more hopeful and more excited than I had ever seen her before and probably more than she had been in quite some time. I figured, though, that I had best remind her that now was not really the time to celebrate. We were a long way from that.

"Miz Lacey."

"Yes, Cowboy?" When she looked up her eyes were alight with eager enthusiasm, and her cheeks were flushed to a healthy, rosy hue with her pleasure. She looked younger and prettier and more alive than at any time since I had arrived here. I kind of hated to burst her bubble so soon.

"Miz Lacey, you have to remember now that this loan won't put you out of the woods, ma'am. It gives you a chance to buy more time, but it won't solve anything by itself, remember. You still have to find and buy those *corrientes* an' slip them across the border without us being shot by Mex rebels or stopped by Mex soldiers or caught by the Border Patrol. An' if you can do all that, it still only buys you another year to try and get the place paying again. I mean, ma'am, there *sure* aren't any guarantees here and nothing's been solved yet. This loan Mr. Abelard is making you is an opportunity, ma'am. It isn't a solution."

"I know that, Cowboy. But oh *my*, isn't it wonderful!"

In spite of my reservations I couldn't help but smile along with her. "Yes, ma'am. It is pretty darn wonderful."

The next morning she had me out cranking the Dort before daylight and after a very short, hurry-up breakfast that she scarcely touched herself and scarcely gave me a chance to.

Mrs. Lacey drove, I think, even faster and wilder than usual, and her usual was plenty fast and wild enough. She took a longer route than I used on horseback, but she sure didn't require as much time to cover it.

Early as we were, Mr. Abelard was ready to receive her. I made the introductions and let Curtis Abelard take over. He was a businessman and an investor, and this was his meat. Without hardly seeming to, he was able to put Mrs. Lacey at ease and explain every step of what he was doing in a clear and simple way so that anyone could have understood it and approved of what was going on.

Inside of a half hour everything was signed, me serving as one witness and Mr. Abelard's cook as the other, and Mrs. Lacey had a cashier's check in her handbag for the full amount promised.

We drank coffee and munched on sweet pastries for a little

while more, but Mrs. Lacey was too wound up to sit still very long. As she was preparing to leave, though, Curtis asked her to wait a moment more.

"Would you mind a word of counsel, Mrs. Lacey?"

"I would welcome it, Mr. Abelard." It was pretty obvious she had taken a liking to him already, and advice from a gentleman of his stature is nothing to sniff away anyhow.

"Thank you," he said, as if it was she who was doing him the favor by listening to him. "Mr. Russel explained some of your plans to me, Mrs. Lacey. In strictest confidence, of course, and as it happens I have had some experience with business dealings across the border. I am familiar with the . . . uh . . . type of person you will be dealing with there.

"You should understand," he said, speaking to her but pointedly glancing my way from time to time now too, "that northern Mexico at the moment is very unstable. There probably will be no way you can really be certain if the people you are dealing with are loyalists or Villistas. And really, for your purposes it will make little or no difference. You won't be advertising your presence in any event.

"I would warn you most strongly, Mrs. Lacey, to not rely on your bank for assistance. A check drawn on any Yankee bank will be unacceptable to most Mexicans and would be outrageously discounted in value by those few who might accept your paper. If you want to strike the best deal possible there, you will have to offer hard specie, not even American currency, and gold rather than silver if at all possible." He smiled. "Gold does have a peculiar appeal of its own that makes it more desirable than the dollar it represents. I daresay you can save fifty cents on a dollar per head if you can offer payment in gold coin.

"Also I would suggest that you not convert a check or cash to gold anywhere near the border. That kind of exchange is much too likely to attract unwanted attention. Secure your gold here and carry it with you." Again the smile. "Carefully."

He got up from his chair and fetched a small valise from beside the desk in the room. "Cowboy, do you happen to own a gun?"

"Good heavens, no," I told him. I'd owned one or two when I was a young buck in Texas and thought that a cowboy should just naturally own a gun, but as I got older I realized that the things are heavy to carry, inaccurate to shoot at any useful distance and much too likely to get lost if your horse gets into a storm or a spooky cow gives you a hard run through the brush. I probably haven't owned a gun in half a dozen years now.

"I thought as much," Curtis said. "If Mrs. Lacey will take my advice, and I certainly hope she will, I would feel much better in my own mind if you were to carry this, Cowboy."

He reached into the bag and pulled out a heavy chunk of a thing that was one of those government .45 automatics like the Army went in for a few years before. It was in a shoulder holster rig that can be hidden under a coat, and he had a couple spare clips with it that he said allowed it to be reloaded in a matter of seconds.

"Are you familiar with these?" he asked.

When I shook my head, he proceeded to show me how to load and operate the ugly thing and how to take it apart and to load the long, seven-shot clips. I dry fired it a few times and parroted back what he had told me until he was satisfied that I could use it all right.

"That isn't your traditional six-gun, Cowboy, but it is dependable and hits like a sledgehammer. And I really will feel better about having advised you if you will carry it."

I gave him my promise and my thanks and accepted the gun from him. I suppose it was only a natural reaction, but I sure felt sobered by the fact of that cold slab of blue metal. Somehow it took away from the excitement and the anticipation I had been feeling and turned the whole venture into something serious if not exactly sinister.

Judging from Mrs. Lacey's expression, Curtis's advice and his gun had had the same effect on her. Despite the presence of that check in her handbag, she was quiet and subdued as we said our good-byes and drove away from there. And I guess I was too.

CHAPTER 19

"Miz Lacey, I've been thinking about this whole thing. 'Specially what all Mr. Abelard said yesterday. I was awake half the night fretting about it."

She put fried ham and poached eggs and some bakery-baked bread on the table and a big crock of fresh butter and a big old jar of strawberry preserves to go with the bread. We were living pretty grand since that trip to see Abelard. "What are you talking about, Cowboy?"

"Carrying all that gold. Him believing I should pack a gun." I shoveled my plate deep with the ham and eggs and a couple slabs of the bread. "What I've been thinking is, this trip could be awful dangerous for you. Down there . . . dealing with foreigners . . . bandits and everything . . . you just never know. It might be safer for you to stay here."

She gave me a *very* odd look. "Are you seriously thinking that I should wait here in Colorado while you take twenty thousand of my gold dollars and go to Mexico with them?"

I grinned at her. "It does sound strange when you put it that way, don't it."

"Strange. That is hardly the word for it. Insane would be more appropriate, I think."

"You won't go for it then, huh?"

"Indeed I will not."

"Okay, then. How about Plan Two?"

"Which is?"

"We both go south, park you and the gold in a hotel this side of the border. I find the seller and bring him to you. You pay him. Then I go back across the border to take delivery of the cattle and bring them out." That was what I was really hoping to get her to agree to. I'd just thrown the other in to give her something to compromise away from, kind of like offering a fellow twenty dollars for a horse he is asking forty for and you'll be willing to buy at thirty.

Again, though, she took no time to think about it before she answered. "I will pay for the cattle when and where I take delivery, Cowboy, and Lord only knows how deep into Mexico that will be. And where those cattle go, *I* go. Every foot of the way."

"Yes, ma'am." There was, of course, nothing I could say about it. The money—and the mortgage—was hers, and I couldn't blame her for wanting to handle it herself. Hell, if her own husband would rob her why wouldn't a drifting hired hand. I wouldn't have, of course, but she couldn't know that. But I had felt obligated to try. Neither of us could know what might happen down south, particularly since that was not country I was familiar with.

I ducked my head and put my attention on my plate. I just sure could have felt easier if I didn't have to worry about her too.

At least Mrs. Lacey did not seem to have been bothered by my suggestion. She might as well not have heard it. "After breakfast we will go in to the city and arrange to pick up the gold coin. Tomorrow if they can get that much on hand by then. Then tomorrow we can pick it up and take the train south. The cattle here should be all right for a few weeks, shouldn't they?"

"They'll have to be. You'll lose a couple heifers and a calf or two, but there shouldn't be any big problems."

She seemed satisfied with that. After all, it was what she wanted to hear. And her cattle here would be all right. *If* there were no windmill failures. *If* there were no grass fires. *If* a lot of things. But there was no point to me bringing those up for her to worry about while she was away. She was putting everything on this one roll of the dice down in Mexico. The rest she didn't need to be distracted by.

I finished my breakfast and shoved the empty plate away. "I'll go crank the auto if you like then, ma'am."

"Please."

At the bank the same old gentleman greeted her and took us into his office. If he was disappointed to have lost out on getting her paper, he sure didn't show it. He seemed genuinely pleased that she had been able to get more money to operate on.

"Naturally we will be glad to accept Abelard's paper," he said. He smiled. "As for converting it to coin, Mrs. Lacey, we can do that this instant if you like. We do supply banking services to the mining districts, you know. Miners customarily take their wages in gold coin. I think you will find our coin supplies ample at all times."

Now that was a thing I had not known. For that matter I hadn't known that there were miners of any kind in the neighborhood. Not that I had any interest in them myself. Anybody ripping into the earth, whether in a mine or with one of those oil drilling rigs, always strikes me as being somehow unnatural. Seeing it makes me a bit queasy in the stomach. Which is beside the point, I suppose.

"Tomorrow morning will do nicely, I think. We will be taking the two thirty-two south."

We left after the appropriate round of social conversation and courtesies. At that point everything seemed to be going just fine.

Mrs. Lacey was feeling positively jubilant. She stopped at a butcher's to buy a chicken for our last supper at the Whiskey, and she was in as good a mood as I had seen her.

The supper ended with something of a bitter aftertaste, though. About the time I was fixing to go from the house back over to the bunkhouse a young fellow knocked at the kitchen door. He had driven out from Monument to deliver a note addressed to me.

Like a damn fool I opened it there in the kitchen. It was from Curtis Abelard.

"Dear Friend Russel," it read. "I dislike being the bearer of bad tidings, but I must strengthen my warning to you to be on your guard. I have reason to believe that Tyler has received word of the lady's plans. I have spoken of her intentions to no one, I assure you, and I doubt you would have. It is possible that my cook may have violated my wishes and mentioned the mortgage signing. It is always possible too that more may have been overheard and repeated. In any event, it is certain that Lonahan has disappeared from the city and that Tyler is most vague about the man's current whereabouts. If I were you, I should be very closely on my guard until the lady's business is successfully concluded. Know that both of you carry my best wishes upon your journey. God speed. Your ob't servant and true friend." It was signed with something of a flourish although the body of the letter he had written in a neat and rather small hand.

Mrs. Lacey must have seen in my face the seriousness of that news. She demanded to know what was up, and after all it was hardly a normal or casual thing for a motor delivery person to bring a note to a hired hand. I let her read it, for she did have a right to know about the danger Lonahan might represent.

We were both in a somber humor when we parted that evening.

CHAPTER 20

If anyone ever wants to know, I am qualified to tell him. A .45 automatic is a heavy damned thing. And a shoulder holster is an awkward damned thing. Worse, it made me feel like some kind of hood, like a highjacker in search of a bootlegger's truck to pirate or one of those scum—Lonahan among them—over in Oklahoma who shot up poor Indians to keep them poor while somebody else got fat off their oil land. On the subject of which, while I don't approve of driving steel for thousands of feet into the earth's gut and would not allow it on any land of mine, I do believe that a fellow has a right to the fruits of his own land if he wants to use it that way. Certainly those oil drillers and claim jumpers don't have any right to take it away from someone, even if he is only an Indian.

Anyway, my whole point is that carrying a gun, particularly a gun hidden under my coat where an honest man wouldn't see it, put me into a strange mood and something of an uneasy one.

Still, I would not have been without it. Not now I wouldn't.

I felt stiff, too, in a high collar and tie—which Mrs. Lacey had insisted that I wear—and rode stiff beside her in the Dort, first to the bank and then—now loaded down by a newly heavy valise—to the railroad depot.

They had Pullman cars on the line, but Mrs. Lacey had gone and ordered a compartment. I thought that something of a hoity-toity extravagance, but maybe she just didn't know there was any other way that respectable people could travel. It did have the practical advantage of privacy, of course, so maybe that and the greater protection for her money were what she was after.

I kept a close watch for Lonahan, but saw no sign of him. I'm not sure what I would or could have done if I had seen him, and I am just as glad I did not. I mean, you don't just go around in public railroad stations these days and gun people down on sight. I sure tried to be watchful anyway.

The train was within six minutes of being on time, which is pretty good considering. We settled in for the run down to Trinidad and the jostling and confusion of hooking on extra engines for the long climb up Raton in the night. Come daylight they remade the train at Santa Fe. Our car was shunted onto a different track and about noon began the long run down to El Paso.

Modern transportation being what it is, we were in Paso by nine-something that night, little more than a day after we left middle Colorado. Not too many years ago that same trip would have taken a couple weeks by a fast horse. Incredible. And one of those flying machines could have left in the morning and been there before dark. The boys who had been Over There said those machines had really become something in the past few years. I hadn't ever seen one myself, but I would kind of like to.

We stayed the night in connecting rooms at, appropriately enough, the Paso del Norte Hotel and in the morning a motor hack had us back at the depot in plenty of time to take the westbound S.P.

There was a world of places where we could have left the train to begin looking for Mex cattle. Since we were not going to be trailing them back up to Colorado and did not have to care about the country that would have to be crossed this side of the border, we could have gone all the way over into Arizona, which traditionally has been a good place to cross cattle into this country.

Mrs. Lacey, though, decided we were going to leave the train at Columbus, New Mexico. So far as I would know her reason for stopping there could have been as simple as the fact that she would have heard of the place before. After all, that's where Villa came across a few years back and killed a bunch of people and got Black-Jack Pershing all stirred up. After all the advances in mechanization they made during the Great War, I would be willing to bet that Pershing's expedition was the last in which the horse cavalry will ever play any real part.

The cav boys with their fancy boots and fancier, flare-sided britches sure were not gone and forgotten, though. There was a bunch of them at the railroad depot when we got off the train and several of them, recognizing a lady when they saw one, made short work of organizing a labor detail to help Mrs. Lacey with her bags. I couldn't help but notice that it was some dashing young officers with shiny bars on their collars who made the offer but a group of enlisted soldiers who did the actual sweating. Oddly enough it was the pair of lieutenants who got all the thank-yous once the bags were deposited in the rooms she took at the hotel. The enlisted boys were given a coin apiece and were sent on their way.

Another thing I noticed, and the truth is that I got a bit of a chuckle out of it, was the size of those khaki-legs.

Now for about as long as I could remember I had heard about the cavalry trooper as being the fighting elite of our military forces. People always talked about them as if they were all eight-foot tall, breathed fire any time they felt like it and could whip any man in the house without spilling their brandy. These boys were all little fellows.

While Mrs. Lacey was enjoying the attentions of the officers I motioned one of the troopers aside and asked him about that, though I was careful to not put it so that he might think I was asking was this an outfit of runts. It turned out that what the Army wanted in its troopers was not big old six-footers but little fellows of 140 pounds give or take a couple. Easier on the horses, and they fit the cavalry issue saddles. I'd never known that.

"Ma'am," I said when our government escort had run out of excuses to linger and finally disappeared, "do you think we might have made a mistake in stopping here?"

"Certainly not. Do you?"

"Well, I couldn't hardly bring it up with those officers here, but what we want to do will be as illegal on this side of the border as it'll be dangerous on the other side, ma'am. This place is smack under the noses of the U. S. Government, ma'am. Don't you think we might do better some place else?"

"Oh dear. I never thought of that. Really. And I've already told Lieutenant Myers and Lieutenant Schrunk that I will be staying here a week or longer. It might seem suspicious if we leave suddenly after my saying that."

"We sure don't want to attract attention. Darn."

"I am sorry," she said. I would not say that she looked entirely disappointed. She'd seemed to enjoy the attentions of those officers. And come to think of it, she had told me that she had first gotten interested in her husband when he was a dashing young cadet on horseback. If she turned out to be uniform crazy, it was her own business, of course, but I sure hoped it would not interfere with our business here.

"What's done is done," I told her. "We'll just have to be that much more careful." I shrugged. "If we're lucky, it will work out that they won't be expecting any cattle smuggling in their own back yard."

"Is that what you would call it, Cowboy? Smuggling? I never thought of it that way exactly, but it does sound exciting, doesn't it?" She seemed quite bright-eyed and enthused actually. Dashing cavalry officers *and* the thrill of becoming a genuine smuggler, all at the same time. Maybe that did something for her. Me it worried.

"I think, ma'am, you should baby-sit the gold this evening while I go across the border and see if I can hear anything interesting."

"Oh, Cowboy, I'm so sorry. I really didn't think. It seems to have been my day for that. I accepted an invitation from those young gentlemen to have dinner with them this evening."

Well, what could I say. It was her damned future we were down here to decide. If she would rather have supper with a flat-hat boy in shiny boots and a wool collar, that was her business.

"You are disappointed with me, aren't you?"

I didn't owe the woman any lies. "Some," I told her.

"You are right to be, of course. I apologize."

"All right."

"I'll make the evening a very short one. The places you will want to visit will be open late, won't they?"

I nodded. A bit grudgingly, I admit, but she was right about that anyway.

To change the subject I asked, "Did you find that pistol that was your daddy's?"

"I have it in my handbag. I don't know that I could hit anything with it."

"As long as it makes a loud noise, it should do all you want it to. You should be safe enough here while I'm gone."

She nodded. I think she was grateful for the change of subject too. "If you don't mind, Cowboy, this has been a tiring trip. I would like to take a nap."

"All right. I'll be just the other side of that door if you need me." I left her alone and went into my connecting room, wishing I had thought to bring a book to read. I would have to correct that oversight the first time I could leave the hotel. As it was, I should have a boring afternoon ahead of me.

CHAPTER 21

There was a collection of shacks on the Mex side of the border and, a couple miles south of that, the town of Las Palomas. A Mexican in a buggy took me down there for fifty cents.

The town wasn't much. But, then, neither was Columbus. I would have to say that I was not overly impressed by this border country. It was even drier than the Texas Panhandle. Sandier and rockier too.

Not that I could see much of Las Palomas when I got there. It was approaching eleven o'clock by then and was several hours past full dark.

I don't know if there is any electric service in the town, but I did not see any in use. The *cantina* the driver took me to and the two others I could see nearby were lighted by oil lamps, and nobody was getting carried away by extravagance in the use of the oil. What they lacked in light they more than made up for in noise though. Going inside was like going swimming, the noise was so thick.

It was sure a cheerful place, though. I will say that about it. The most of the noise was coming from a three-piece band. I couldn't say how good they were, but they got high marks for vigor. The rest of the noise was from people trying to talk loud enough to be heard over the music. There wasn't anybody dancing but there was a space eight or ten feet square left clear. Everybody seemed too busy talking and drinking for that, I guess. And they did seem to be having a fine time. If anybody here was upset about the part-time war going on around here, I couldn't tell it from watching.

I waded through the crowd to the bar and held up a finger. I hadn't any idea what I was ordering, but since I didn't speak the local language it would have to do. The barman brought me a small glass of a clear liquor and a larger glass that looked to be a cloudy home-brewed beer. I hated to be doing any drinking here, but I had to have some excuse for being in the place. I gave myself several stern warnings to go slow and then knocked the liquor back. It tasted pretty good in spite of the lack of color. The barman took fifteen cents out of the change I laid on the counter and I motioned for another.

An hour or so later I was feeling pretty good and didn't care a bit that I couldn't understand what anybody was saying. My lips and cheeks were feeling just a wee bit numb, and I reminded myself that I was here on business. A little fresh air was what I needed, I decided.

I went outside and sat on the plank stoop that ran along the front of the building. The music sounded pretty good from there. Oddly enough it had been a while since I remembered actually hearing it, although they must have been playing right along.

A heavy-set Mexican came outside and went down to the other end of the porch. He belched loudly and made water into the dirt. He turned and walked back toward my end of the stoop, fumbling to refasten his trousers as he did. He burped again, loudly sighed his satisfaction and sat down beside me. He was smiling happily.

"You are alone?" he asked.

I nodded. "Don't speak Spanish either."

"That is a shame."

"You sure speak English good."

His smile got wider at the compliment. "I have done much work in the north. Since I was small I have done this."

"What kind of work do you do?"

He shrugged and said something in Spanish. From the tone of it if it didn't mean "this and that," it should have.

"Actually, I was kind of hoping you were a *vaquero*," I told him.

"Ah, *vaquero*. Good work. Very good work." He grinned.

"Very low pay. Not for me. You want to hire *vaqueros?* Work your cows maybe?"

Now it was my turn to grin. "Not me. I don't own any cows. Not yet. I'd like to get some though."

He didn't take the bait, though. "You need a good saddle? Maybe boots? I work very good with"—he searched for the word momentarily, which made me wonder about his level of experience, at least north of the border—"with the leather."

"No, I have about everything I need in that line."

"A . . . *jacimira* then. I make them very good. Rawhide core. Good braid. Yes?"

"No." At first I didn't catch what he meant, but as he went on I guessed it as a hackamore.

"*La reata?* Very good braid. Very heavy. Fly through the brush. Catch every damn cow, every damn throw. Very cheap."

I shook my head. "Thanks, but I don't work in the brush country. Way up north. Nothing there but grass and wind. We use grass ropes there. Longer than your rawhide lariats. Lighter. Cheaper too."

"You change your mind you let me know." He stood and offered his hand, so I stood up and took it. He shook very solemnly. "You need anything you let me know. I can get it cheap."

"Steers. I need some steers."

He smiled and shrugged his shoulders. "With rawhide I cannot make a steer."

"No."

He gave me a nod which he delivered with such dignity and formality that he made it seem more like a bow. *"Con Dios,* my friend."

"And you, amigo."

He smiled and touched me on the shoulder. "So you do know some of my language. That is good." He gave my shoulder a sharp squeeze and turned to walk with a drinking man's caution back into the *cantina.*

Well, I shouldn't have expected it to be that easy. I sat back down and did some deep breathing. My lips still felt numb.

"Nothing?"

"No, ma'am." I felt kind of queasy and really did not appreciate being dragged out of bed after a couple skimpy hours of sleep. Being faced now with greasy bacon and grease-swimming fried mush did not help at all. "I talked to a couple people. Didn't do any good." I eyed the food, pushed my plate away and settled for coffee. Even that wasn't very appetizing. "I'll go down there again this afternoon."

"I accepted a luncheon engagement for today. You can go back across the border when I return from that."

"Yes, ma'am."

I caught myself—I hoped it hadn't carried over into my voice disapproving of her accepting an "engagement" again, probably with one of those young cav officers.

The way I was regarding that, my being critical of her, of course, was because she was a married woman. But shoot, her husband had taken off on her and robbed her in the bargain. He was certainly no bargain himself. And the truth is that if she hadn't been a lady, I mean if she was just any yahoo's woman, no one would have thought a thing about it if she had chosen to go somewhere else and make a new and better life for herself.

As a lady and the last of an old and fine family, though, she was being held in place by the land she was trying so hard to save and was being held as well by the social obligations of her family and her position. In the public's eye and in mine too she was expected to act above what would have been understood, if not openly allowed, in anyone else.

That was wrong, of course. To go by one set of standards for most folks and a different and harder standard for people like Mrs. Lacey could not be right.

I understood all that well enough. But I sure felt the disapproval just the same. Damnit, a married woman has no business seeing men socially.

If she did sense anything of what I was feeling, she didn't comment on it or try to explain herself to me. She concentrated on the breakfast that had been spread on a table in her room.

"I wonder," she said idly after a few minutes, "if perhaps I should put that cash into the hotel safe."

"I gave that some thought myself, ma'am," I told her. "If we were back at that big, fine hotel in El Paso, I would say yes. This place, well, I don't know as I'd want to trust so much to just anybody's care or just any safe. I understand there are specialists who can open some safes as easy as you or I could open a door."

She sighed. "I suppose you are right. All morning I have been telling myself I am being silly to be suspicious and untrusting, but I *have* felt a certain reluctance to let the money out of sight. All right, Cowboy, we will keep it here where we can watch it then. It just would have been so much easier otherwise."

"Easier it would have been, but I'm not sure about it being safer, and that's what really counts. Look, will you be needing me for a while?"

"Not for several hours. Why?"

"I'd just like to go out for a while. Pick up a book to read for whenever I have to be up here in the room. Like that."

"That will be fine. I don't need to go anywhere until Lieutenant Myers calls for me."

"All right, ma'am. I'll see you later then." I went back into my own room and got my coat. It was plenty hot country down here but I needed the suitcoat to cover the .45 in its shoulder holster. Fortunately, most fellows down here were still respectable enough to believe they weren't properly dressed to be in town if they weren't wearing a coat, so I wouldn't be conspicuous for wearing it.

I was noticing that a lot of young fellows were beginning to show up on the public streets in their vests and shirt-sleeves and some with just their shirts on. It used to be that only farmers would be seen in public that way, but no longer. I believe the war had had something to do with that, maybe by so many soldiers getting used to uniforms that most of the time were just shirts and trousers. I really think the khaki shirt had a lot to do with that trend.

Anyway, I put my coat on and locked the hotel room door behind me and went out onto the street.

A few minutes of cruising the several blocks of the business district showed no signs advertising a bookseller's shop, so I tried the nearest of the several general mercantiles in the town.

There was a small rack of books near the front door which I began to look over to see if anything caught my eye. I had been there four or five minutes, I guess, when a very elegantly dressed Mexican came into the place.

He was a young fellow, built very slim, and was wearing a short jacket and narrow-legged trousers and a hat with less crown and more brim than anything I had ever seen before. His boots were tall and beautifully made. Judging from the stitching on them and the inlays of different colors of leather I would have bet that his boots alone would cost half a year's wages. The other half could have gone for the silver band around the crown of his hat.

He was wearing long-shanked spurs with rowels a good two inches across. The rowels scraped the floor when he walked.

Shoot, if this wasn't a genuine *vaquero* I probably never would see one. I put down the book I'd been looking at and began to sidle over toward him.

CHAPTER 22

"Yes, I speak English quite well, thank you. Do you speak Spanish?"

"I'm afraid not."

"A pity," he said. I couldn't quite decide if he was trying to be ugly about it. "What is it you want of me?"

"Well now, you look like a cowman to me, and I happen to be looking for some steers. I just thought it might be worthwhile for the two of us to have a little talk, that's all."

He sniffed. In a common man you might have called it more of a snort, but this fellow was too much of a dandy to be caught being common. "I have nothing to do with cows, I assure you. Only with the black bulls of the *ganderia*. You do not know of the *ganderia*, gringo? Of course not." The rascal never did explain that, and I never did find out what he was talking about.

"I am a *charro*," he went on haughtily. "But a *vaquero*? Pah! I am also very busy, and it is obvious we will do no business together. You will please excuse me." It was no question.

He turned away and motioned to the storekeeper, who obviously knew him. The storeman, an American of course, got a steel lock-box from under the counter and pulled out a very small, velvet-covered box that the Mex took and without looking inside the box paid for it with a very thick wad of American currency. The storekeeper dropped the money into the lock-box without bothering to count it. They exchanged some pleasantries in Spanish and the Mex left without dawdling.

I guess I was kind of caught rubbernecking at them. When the Mex was gone the storeman gave me a smile and a wink. "Don't mind Raoul," he said. "You just have to understand that he's a bastard and let it go at that. Everybody around here does."

"Is he as rich as he acts?" I asked, moving over to the counter.

"Richer," the man said. He laughed. "That's why everyone around here accepts him the way he is. The rest of the family's pretty nice though. They own a bunch of mines below the border and spend a bunch of money on this side of it."

The man tilted his head to one side and gave me a looking over. After a moment he said, "You were asking about cattle. Would it be Mex cattle you'd be looking for?"

I shrugged. "I'm looking for some cheap cattle. Just put it that way."

He grinned. "Mex cattle then. It's a pity about the border bein' closed for the beef trade. Used to be a good business around here. There's dip vats and a official U. S. Gov'ment inspection station over west of town. Closed now, of course. It used to stay real busy."

"Uh-huh," I said casually. "Of course, if I found a good deal on some Mexican cattle I could always hold them south of the border while they feed out to top weight. Gamble on the border being open again in a year or two. Fella might make a decent profit that way." Which was the story I had worked out in my head before I ever started putting feelers out.

"That's a thought," the man said. "You couldn't hardly lose money—unless the Villistas messed with you—and you could stand to gain quite a bit if they opened up at just the right time. Be all right for a man who didn't mind a gamble," he said. He also winked. He didn't believe a word of it, of course, but it was a nice story anyhow.

"You . . . uh . . . wouldn't have any ideas on the subject, would you?"

He winked once again. Any more and I was going to think he had a twitch. "As a matter of fact, I was just going to say that I might have a suggestion or two. You . . . uh . . . couldn't stop back by here in the morning, could you? After I'd have time to talk to a person or two?"

"I guess I'll still be around."

He gave me a real thorough looking over while trying to pretend that he wasn't. "I'll see you tomorrow," he said shortly. He turned away and began fussing with the stock on a shelf behind the counter. I noticed that he hadn't given me his name nor asked for mine.

That was all right if that was what he wanted. I still needed a book to read but I could sure look for one elsewhere. I left the store without a lot of chummy good-byes.

"You found your book, I see," Mrs. Lacey said when I got back.

"Uh-huh. Might've found your cattle too."

Well *that* got her attention.

"No," I told her, "don't get excited yet. It could be a complete bust. I'll know more tomorrow."

"Tell me . . ." She was interrupted by a knock at the door.

"Miss Turnbull?" It was the lieutenant's voice. He sounded awfully young. Awfully eager too.

I guess I couldn't help looking at her, and I guess I couldn't help raising my eyebrows some. "Miss Turnbull?" I asked, with a slightly different meaning from when the lieutenant asked it.

"It *is* my name, you know," she whispered. Louder she said, "Just a minute. I'll be right there." She dropped back to a whisper. "Take the money, Cowboy, and go into your own room, all right? And don't forget a thing that happened this morning. I want to hear all of it. Go on now. Wait. Here, you forgot your book."

"Thanks," I whispered back at her. I just barely stopped myself short of winking at her. Whatever that darn storekeeper had it seemed to be catching. I took the book and the bag and my curiosity and slipped quietly into my own room.

CHAPTER 23

Mrs. Lacey—Miss Turnbull down here—wanted awful bad to come with me, but one of us had to keep an eye on that bag of money. So midmorning the next day I was by myself when I went up the three steps to the porch and into the store.

My man wasn't behind the counter. Instead there was a woman there. I looked around to make sure I was in the right place.

The woman looked me over and said, "You'd be Mr. Russel." It was a statement of fact spoken without emphasis or apparent welcome. It was also very interesting. I hadn't given my name yesterday, but that did not seem to have slowed them down much. I wondered what else they might know about me that I didn't know about them.

"That's me," I said cheerfully. I was feeling just a little bit nervous but hoped I was hiding that. "I was kind of expecting to see someone else here today."

The woman nodded. "He's waiting for you at the house. Do you know where it is?"

I shook my head and refrained from asking the obvious. Criminy, I didn't know these people's names much less where they lived.

She gave me directions to the place; it was only a block and a half away. "He'll be waiting for you in the kitchen. That's the door in the back. Just go on in. No need to be formal."

I thanked her and made my way down the side street the way she had told me. The house was small and like most town places was awful close to its neighbors. There was a mailbox on the gate post, though, with the name Wyman on it. Knowing just that little bit was knowing a lot more than I had before. I let myself through the gate and went around back to the kitchen door. Wyman was waiting for me inside. So were two Mexicans.

Both Mexicans were well fed and neatly dressed in business suits. There were some Panama skimmer hats on the table beside them. Certainly neither of these men was my idea of what a Mexican cowman would look like. Neither of them rose or offered a hand when I came in, but they did nod.

Wyman said something to them in rapid Spanish. The only part of it I understood was my own name. He turned to me then and said, "These gentlemen, Mr. Russel, have some cattle available below the border. They are Señor Alvarez"—the one to my right nodded—"and Señor Romero."

I waited but the other fellow didn't so much as flick his eyes. There was a quick scraping sound, as of a foot moving on the floor, and the man brightened up and pointed to himself. I damn near broke out laughing. He'd gone and forgotten what name they had given him and it sure wasn't his own. Alvarez, by far the sharper looking of the two, looked somewhat apologetic.

"Have a seat, Mr. Russel," Wyman said.

"Sure. Thanks." I took my time about hanging my hat on a stand beside the door and choosing a chair across the table from the Mexicans, next to Wyman. I gave both the Mexes a looking over and decided the one pretending to be Romero was wearing something mighty bulky at about the same place my own .45 hung. If these were your average, everyday Mexican cattlemen, then I was a Tulsa roughneck with grease under my fingernails.

Alvarez spoke next. "My good friend Mr. Wyman tells us you are thinking of buying beef cattle, yes?"

I nodded. Alvarez smiled. He was missing a couple of teeth just to the left of center. His smile made him look a much rougher fellow than he had seemed a moment before.

"You will please excuse my friend Romero," Alvarez said. "He speaks no English."

"No need for excuses," I said. "He speaks at least as much English as I do Spanish."

"*Bueno,*" Alvarez said. "A good . . ." He seemed to be groping.

"Attitude?" Wyman suggested.

Alvarez smiled. "Yes. Good." He clapped his hands together sharply. "What is it you want, Mr. Russel?" So much for chit-chat.

"Steers. Mid-weights; what we would call feeder steers."

He nodded as if he understood what I meant all right. "Two years old is good?"

"Or three," I said. *Corrientes* run small and are slow to develop, I knew. I had worked some of them in Texas though not many. They were more common over in Arizona, I'd heard.

Again Alvarez nodded. "How many?"

"That depends on the price. I only have a limited amount to spend."

Alvarez pulled a notepad and pencil from his coat pocket. He began drawing squiggly lines on the paper. Killing time while he did some thinking, I decided. "Twelve dollars," he said.

"No."

He seemed to be waiting for me to go on, but I wasn't in any hurry.

"Such steers are worth much more over here," he said.

"They aren't over here," I told him. "They can't be brought over here. That's your own law, after all."

"Of course." He doodled on his pad some more. "Bank drafts. Very hard to cash in my country. Very slow. Much tax. Many questions."

"I pay in hard money. Gold coin. A small amount in currency." Mrs. Lacey didn't know about the currency. That was mine, in a money belt under my shirt.

Alvarez began to look more interested. His eyes moved to Wyman and quickly back, but not so quickly that Wyman didn't catch it too.

Wyman said something to him in Spanish, and Alvarez's response, I thought, was a bit hot. They began to go back and forth and a couple of times I heard the word *dinero.* I don't know if that is a genuine Spanish word but it is a common Tex-Mex term for money.

I was beginning to be amused now, and to cover it while they scrapped I got up and helped myself to a cup of Wyman's coffee although none had been offered.

Wyman's part in this was becoming clear now. It would have been his job to convert a draft into real money, probably for a fat bite of it. Now the need for Mr. Wyman was thinned down considerable. Their business, of course. So long as it didn't interfere with mine.

I took my coffee back to the table and waited them out. When they were done Wyman didn't look too happy.

"Gold?" Alvarez asked.

"And a small amount of currency," I told him.

"Most in gold?"

"About twenty to one."

He definitely looked pleased. "Nine dollars," he said.

"Six-fifty."

We were into it for fair now. Oh, he did groan and fuss and carry on. He called on his mother and both his sainted grandmothers to observe how grossly he was being insulted. He lapsed into Spanish and back to English. He clutched his bodyguard by the arm and complained loudly to him in both languages, including the one the man did not speak.

The thing was, we had a deal working here. We had a lot of details to work out yet, but we definitely had something going now.

He would consent to take $8.75.

I would consider that if he would deliver the herd at Las Palomas and give me complete cut-back privileges to reject whatever I didn't like.

Impossible. I was breaking his heart.

You bet I was. This guy had to be a Villista. In Las Palomas the Federales would grab those cattle and return them to whoever used to own them and shoot the *vaqueros* for good measure.

Impossible. The cattle were sixty miles below the border. His *vaqueros* were very, very busy. He could not possibly spare them to bring the herd north.

They were worth much less to me down there although it was true, of course, that I intended to leave the herd in Mexico. Seven dollars per head if they were to be delivered so far away.

You'd have thought I'd stabbed him in the heart. He probably would have reacted less if I *had* stabbed him. He sought consolation from his friend. There could be no consolation for such a thing. Seven dollars, indeed.

Eight-fifty, perhaps.

Impossible. Now it was my turn to groan some. He wanted to take advantage of a poor man who dreamed of seeing his own small herd of beeves on the sweet, green grass of the good earth. I thought I put on quite a show. I offered seven and a quarter.

We went on like that for quite some time. In the end we agreed that he was to be paid $7.75 per head and I was to keep cut-back privileges. He would make available a herd of—I borrowed his pad and pencil to do some figuring—3,400 head. I would cut back any I did not want and keep probably 2,500 to 3,000 head. The 3,000 figure would be beyond our budget, but he didn't have to know that. The more he expected me to buy, the better quality he was likely to bring along and the fewer culls.

"And how will you pay?" Alvarez asked.

I looked at him and knew damned good and well that this nicely dressed Mexican businessman across the table from me was a bandit and maybe much worse. If Mrs. Lacey and I rode sixty miles down into Mexico with him knowing we were carrying gold, it was very likely that we neither of us would live to see that herd of *corriente* steers. That would be awfully convenient for the Villistas but not so great for us.

I had an absolute brainstorm and gave him a broad smile.

"You'll be paid here," I told him. "My partner and I will give you an exact number of steers. Forget that 2,500 to 3,000 figure. We'll work out what we want and pay you for them here. You count the money and lock it into a bag. The bag we will put into a vault at the bank with instructions that it is to be released to you only when all three of us come back to claim it. I hope you understand my caution. I intend no disrespect."

He grinned. *"Bueno.* I like you, Mr. Russel."

"And I've enjoyed doing business with you, Señor Alvarez."

We were very good friends now. And it was definitely in the Villistas' best interests for us to return to Columbus intact. We might have to be afraid of a lot of things down south, but not of Pancho and his boys.

I stood and offered my hand, and we parted the best of friends. Except possibly for Wyman. If he was going to end up with a piece of this he was going to have to hammer it out of Alvarez or whatever the man's name really was. But that was his problem.

"Good day, gentlemen."

"Until tomorrow," Alvarez said.

CHAPTER 24

Alvarez and Romero, or whoever they were, knocked on my hotel room door promptly at 2 P.M. the next day. The door to Mrs. Lacey's room was closed but not locked. They probably already knew about her. Wyman or someone had certainly done some checking on me after our first conversation. Still, there was no point in waving her at them like a flag.

The business we had to conduct that day was short and simple. We agreed to take and to pay for 2,850 head of steers at $7.75 per head, 2,700 to be bought with gold coin and 150 with currency. The 150 were mine.

Alvarez surprised me and made me regard them as much more efficient than I would have suspected. No *mañana* boy this one. He would send a rider as soon as the money was paid, to insure that the herd would be available for us. Would four days be convenient for us to find our crew and meet his *vaqueros?*

It would, I thought.

Then as soon as the money could be paid. . . . He waited expectantly.

Of course. I rapped lightly on the connecting door. When she answered the knock Mrs. Lacey looked nervous and perhaps a bit scared. She bore up just fine during the introductions.

Alvarez, I noticed, seemed not at all surprised to see that my partner was a woman. I was sure that he had already known about her.

I got our heavy valise and we all walked together to the town's one bank. Mrs. Lacey's ladylike presence helped a great deal there, I believe. They gave us a private room where we could make the transfer and assured us—assured her, really—that our instructions for vault storage and release would be fully followed. I gathered that strange dealings with Mexican businessmen might not be much of a novelty here.

The money was quickly enough counted out and placed back into the valise. What Mrs. Lacey had left fit handily enough into her purse. The bills I had left would not make much of a bulge in my pocket.

Alvarez, at least, was all smiles. Curtis Abelard's advice had been right on the button. The appeal of hard, shining gold had made a big difference to him. When those double eagles were stacked on the table in tall, yellow piles Alvarez's eyes had positively glowed.

The money belonged to him now or soon would. The Villistas would, I suspected, use it to buy weapons or ammunition to continue their years-long revolution against Mexican civil authority. But that was the problem of the Federales, thank goodness, and not mine. We shook hands and watched the valise being locked into the bank's steel vault. They would release it again only to the three of us, in person, although Alvarez had the privilege of sending an agent if he wished.

From now on Alvarez and the Villistas had more than 22,000 good reasons for Mrs. Lacey and me to remain healthy and unharmed.

I sure felt better once that was done.

Lining up a crew was no problem down here. There were enough fellows on the loose, boys who had come south looking for easy roads to big money with fighting going on so near, that I could pretty much pick and choose the people I wanted.

As a matter of fact, after I'd hired the first three of the six I figured we would need I was being approached by volunteers. One of them offered to pay *me* for the privilege of going along. He was a newspaper reporter, though, and likely could not have hit the ground by accident if he happened to drop his rope.

I turned him down, of course, but afterward I got to thinking about him being so anxious to go with us. Obviously, it was no big secret that Mrs. Lacey and I were going south to deal with the Villistas. And if some chucklehead from a Chicago newspaper had heard about it, more than likely the Army had too.

Anyway, I did find a crew. Two dollars a day and they supplied their own horses. I found a cook, too, with his own pack mules who agreed to come for four dollars a day and a quart of border booze when we got back.

Mrs. Lacey in the meanwhile was a pack of nerves, although why she should choose now to get nervous I could not totally understand. The time to be nervous, to my mind, was when we were alone in that room with the money and Alvarez and Romero. Then and when we brought the herd up to the border for the crossing.

She was so darn wound up, though, that she had begged off from her cavalry officer friends and was no longer Miss Turnbull but was back to being Mrs. Lacey full time.

Somehow, mostly by sitting and fretting, she made it through until the appointed hour, and the whole crew of us gathered at the livery where I had rented horses for Mrs. Lacey and me to ride. We didn't cross the border right off, not with what was so obviously a riding crew. Instead we rode east along the S.P. tracks.

About five miles from town a group of Mex riders, four of them there were, appeared without warning out of a clump of dense mesquite near the right of way. If I'd thought we had anything to fear from Mexican bandits, they would have scared me half silly. As it was I had to jump quick to soothe some unsettled nerves among the crew.

Alvarez was not among this bunch but his buddy Romero was. The leader of the pack introduced himself as Julio. No last name given. We were to follow him, he said.

And you know all those wild imaginings about Mexican bandits being loaded down with bandoliers of cartridges and several pistols and carbines slung all over them and their animals?

Believe it. They really were.

We turned south and a few minutes later were across the border and into Old Mexico.

CHAPTER 25

More of the Villistas joined us as we moved south, a pair here and a trio appearing out of the brush somewhere else, until there were twenty-five of them. Enough to make up a sizable fighting force if the need should arise.

That fact and one other that I could not help but soon notice as we rode brought home to me the fact that this was a warfaring land we were passing through. Up until that time, really, the idea of Mexican bandits was to me really pretty much like an idea presented on a comic-opera stage. It was interesting; it was amusing in a manner of speaking; but it wasn't quite real.

Now the sheer numbers of the men who were escorting us made it come closer to reality.

The clincher, though, the thing that truly made me feel and accept their fight as a reality for them, was the desert we were riding through. And I am really not meaning now the dry and rocky land itself, although it was by far the nearest thing to a true desert that I had ever ridden—though it is true too that on much of what people call a desert you find a good deal of edible forage which to my mind merely makes it grazing rather than farming country.

What I mean by desert here is the lack of human contact we found as we rode through.

This was a populated area, mind. There were towns a few miles distant. We crossed several roads, one of them quite good, and many trails and wagon paths.

The country was full of the tracks and the droppings of domestic goats and sheep, and there were a few cattle about.

From time to time we could see a collection of *jacals* and, less often, a small *rancheria*. These places had gardens scratched into the soil and springs or hand-dug wells nearby. At several I could see clothing spread or hung to dry after washing.

Yet nowhere did we see a single living person beyond our own party.

No children played in the shade near these houses. No women peered suspiciously from the empty doorways. No men stepped forward to inquire of our business or to offer us welcome. In terms of the people who lived here, we were truly passing through a desert land.

We stopped the night at one of the empty *rancherias*, and we Americans were offered the use of the principal house. Mrs. Lacey gave Julio an odd look and shook her head no. She might have been too weary to speak to him, but I did not think it was that at all.

I glanced inside the house. There was a bucket on the table and some crockery dishware stacked beside it. A piece of sacking had been tossed onto the table, probably where someone had been drying dishes. There was still a slightly darkened damp area on the sacking. And in such dry country any moisture would not long remain. Whoever lived here was probably out in the brush right now, watching and worrying about what was going to happen to their place. No way was I going to go inside and make myself to home there knowing that.

Our crew and Mrs. Lacey made a camp beside the garden at Mrs. Lacey's insistence. I think she did that on purpose so the Mexicans would more likely stay clear of it and not trample down the beans and the peppers and the bit of corn growing there.

She was so tired she was gray-faced and was very pale at the corners of her mouth. When she got off her rented horse she'd been wobble-kneed and unsteady, but I never heard her complain about any of it. Maybe if there had been another woman in the party she would have felt freer to express her feelings or admit to fatigue, but as it was she gritted her teeth and toughed it out.

Fortunately, we didn't have to feed the whole crowd that was traveling with us. Our cook provided for our own people from the things we had brought along. The Mexicans fended for themselves. I could not help noticing, though, that the *rancheria* was fresh out of chickens before they were done. None of us said anything to them about it, I must admit.

Come morning we were on our way early—no doubt to the great relief of the *rancheria* owner and his family—and reached the cattle by late morning.

Julio rode over beside Mrs. Lacey and me when we came in sight of the herd.

"Just as we promised," he said. He seemed pretty proud of the bunch and waved an arm toward the steers in a gesture sweeping enough for ten times the number to be spread out before him.

"Yes they are. Thank you," Mrs. Lacey agreed.

Me, I held off judgment until we were near enough for me to get a proper look at the beeves. When we were I told him, "I got to admit it, Julio. You boys put together a real decent bunch of steers here, 'specially on such short notice. They're better than I looked for."

"We treat our friends very well," Julio said. "You maybe want to do business with us again."

"Could be," I told him. And it was tempting, too. A fellow could pick up a herd of stock cows awful cheap this way. The thing was, we came down here with cash and so we were their friends. These steers probably were donated to Villa's cause by their enemies, and even though I had never given any thought to one side over another in this long-running Mexican fuss, I hated the idea of someone losing his herd so that I could have mine. It was tempting in a way, but not so much so that I was willing to do it again.

Whoever had put this herd together, though, had done a nice job of it. They were reasonably uniform in size, all of them five hundred to five-fifty pounds per head, and they looked healthy. None of them showed any of the modern breed bloodlines in them but having been raised slowly on the rough forage this country had to offer they would do well when they were put onto full feed in a commercial feed lot, which was almost certainly where they would go.

I circled the herd to look them all over and saw that a buyer could almost take herd-run from them and not be hurt. The cutback privilege I'd been so worried about was not a big thing now. What was more, they had brought nearly 4,000 head for us to pick from.

In a lot of ways I just couldn't quite decide if I liked these fellows or if I ought to despise them. I guess like anyone else these Villistas were neither all black nor all white but shades in between. And if I ever met anyone from the other side I would probably find that true of them too.

Anyway, Mrs. Lacey and the cook set up a camp near a slow-flowing seep where we could water the stock, and the crew and I set about pulling out the beeves we wanted.

Julio even had some of his people hold the cut for us while the Mex *vaqueros* who had been with the herd when we arrived continued in charge.

With all seven of us, the six hands and me, pulling steers out and with so few of them to be culled the work went quickly and we had what I thought we needed by dark. A formal tally would have to wait for morning, but I figured we had closer to 2,900 in our bunch than the 2,850 we'd paid for. Julio got my approval first and then had four of the *vaqueros* drive the cutbacks off into the dark somewhere.

"If you would like," he said, "my people, they can hold your herd for the night. Give you a rest before we start."

That was a damned generous offer even if the steers were still properly his until a count was made, and I thanked him appropriately. So did the hands. Those boys were pulling their pay mighty easy so far.

Julio joined us for supper—the least we could do in exchange for his courtesy—and we all turned in early.

Some silly son-of-a-bitch was rattling my brains and hissing a stream of fast Spanish into my ear. I came up off my bedroll fast.

"Calm down," I told him. "You speak any English?"

"*Si.*"

"Good. Try it." Something was pretty obviously wrong, but I didn't know what. If those beeves had jumped into a run, I would have heard it and come awake before anybody could have come to tell me about it, and I would have been hearing it now too. The night was quiet except for the sounds of men moving around the cinch straps being pulled tight. "What is it, man?"

"Move. Must move now."

"Why?"

He was groping for it but I guess he didn't have enough English to get to where he wanted to go.

Julio appeared at his side and told the fellow something, and he took off at a run.

"We must move now," Julio said. "My people are with the cows, *si?* They will meet us later. Now we must go."

I was beginning to understand. "Federales?"

Julio spread his hands and shrugged. Which I took to mean that he did not necessarily want to tell me, but probably yes.

"Our horses aren't saddled," I told him. We hadn't gone to the expense of bringing a remuda for such a short drive, and you can't leave an animal under saddle day and night.

"My people are doing that now."

"All right." I turned and began kicking the boys out of their beds. Mrs. Lacey I wakened a little more gently.

"What is it, Cowboy?" At least she was not an extra-heavy sleeper.

I told her, both what I knew and what I guessed.

"What about the cattle?"

"They'll meet us with them later. Their first concern is to keep us safe. Otherwise they don't get paid."

"You think we should trust them?"

"Ma'am, we have a clean choice about that, it's true, but if we guess wrong here, we could land in a Mex jail. After the stories I've heard on that subject, ma'am, I do figure to trust these boys myself. Indeed I do."

She nodded and did some wiggling under her blankets, getting herself rebuttoned and decent I guessed. She wasn't slow once she got to it.

A couple of the hands were already helping the cook pull his packs together, and we were ready by the time the Villistas rode up leading our horses.

"Stay close to me," Julio said, "and do not worry about the trail. I know the way, so trust to your horse and do not slow us down."

That sounded ominous as could be but by then we were off at a high lope and soon were riding harder.

The Mexes, I noticed, were formed up all around us with most of them immediately to our rear. Several of them were riding with rifles in their hands.

CHAPTER 26

By dawn we were at least a dozen miles away and for more than an hour had been waiting—hiding really—in a circle of rock that should have concealed us from anyone outside of rock-chunking distance.

"When can we leave and where are my cattle?" Mrs. Lacey demanded of Julio.

"Soon we can leave. Tomorrow we will join the cattle," he said patiently. Her annoyance did not seem to ruffle him at all. He climbed one of the rocks and looked slowly around the empty countryside. He motioned first to one of his men and then to another.

The two flowed smoothly into their saddles without using the stirrups, pulled their rifles from their scabbards and rode out.

"We may move soon," Julio said when he came back to where we were waiting.

The two men had not needed detailed instructions from their leader, no more so than a good hand would need when you put him on a gather. They seemed to know what was required and how to do it. All of a sudden I was beginning to think of Julio and his men as soldiers instead of just bandits.

We had a cold breakfast of tortillas and dried beef that the Villistas supplied. We sure hadn't thought to bring anything suitable for use without cooking fires.

One of the scouts came back after about forty-five minutes. His report to Julio was no more than a nod, so it must have been clear out there. The other one was back five minutes or so later. He spoke to Julio, but of course it was in Spanish.

Julio hollered something and turned to us Americans. "We go now."

The cinches were drawn tight again and we rode out of the protection of the rocks.

I was traveling beside Mrs. Lacey and once everyone was going easy Julio moved in near us. Across Mrs. Lacey—Julio seemed to regard me as the trail boss or something—he said, "You will be happy to know that your cattle are safe. The *vaqueros* were able to persuade the soldiers that we bad ones took some of the herd and went south." He did not look pleased in spite of that report.

"Your people," I asked him. "Are they all right?"

He gave me a sudden hard, questioning look.

"You act pretty grim for a man who says everything is just fine," I explained.

"The Federales are not easily convinced," he said. "One must let them convince themselves that they hear the truth. One of our *vaqueros*," he shrugged, "he did not survive the questioning. The Federales were so moved by regret that they left the dead man's things for his friends to share."

Again he shrugged. "At least now they will not think it strange that the *vaqueros* move the herd away from that place." He gave us a very bitter smile that was more grimace than grin. "We are a very primitive and superstitious people, you know."

"What about the people driving the small herd? Won't the soldiers follow them?"

"Yes." He let it go at that.

"Will they be all right?" Mrs. Lacey persisted.

"Only God knows such things." Julio lightly touched the steel to his horse and moved away. He made a great show of having to position his men, but I am certain he just wanted to end our questions. Perhaps the words were scraping on bone now.

We rode west and a little south and spent the night in a shallow pocket where a creek flowed for perhaps three hundred yards before it disappeared into a patch of damp, sandy soil. The hollow was green and almost lush in appearance, holding a grove of large trees and some flowering plants as well. Until I saw those trees I hadn't realized how long it had been since I had seen one. Or how much I missed them.

It was a pleasant spot there, and we stayed until late the following day when the cattle reached us.

"We can go on at once if you wish or let the cattle water and rest here overnight," Julio said.

"Let them rest," I told him. "And I believe it's our turn to stand the night watch while your people sleep."

He smiled and said something in Spanish. From his tone of voice I was thinking it would have been something nice.

Come morning we ate—a regular meal complete with a cooking fire and everything—and began trailing the herd north. The *vaqueros* stayed with us and so did Julio and his soldiers, though they were ranging pretty far out from the cattle and making no attempt to help work the herd. It was pretty obvious that they were acting strictly as a bodyguard here.

Julio figured it would take us four days to make the border, and on the fourth morning he told us we were just ten miles short of it. Now I was not what you would call lost. I knew darn good and well that the good old U.S. was due north of wherever we might be so if we just kept going until we found the S.P. tracks we would be all right. Still, I really hadn't had any idea of exactly where we were in relation to the border.

"We cross back over to our side this afternoon," I told the boys. "So be sharp today, and after the noon stop we'll want to take them plenty slow. We don't want any dust clouds telling the world where we are. No more than we can help anyhow."

Mrs. Lacey gave me a smile that was tight enough to make it clear she was playing pretend. She was plenty worried, as well she should be. Below the border any squabble with the government really wasn't our worry, and if the Mexes didn't like what we were doing that was just too bad.

Above the line though, well, those were our own troopers who might find us and raise an objection. If that happened, we could have a border incident on our consciences at best. Or the lives of some khaki-clad boys to account for at the worst. We sure didn't want that.

We trailed the herd north again through the unbroken miles of scrub land, unmarked in this particular area by roads or rails or signs of the *jacals* and *rancherias* we had seen elsewhere. I had to give Julio credit for picking his route well. But then maybe they had used it before for other purposes.

We nooned at a dry camp in the brush and again went without fires, the Mexicans handing out a sort of rolled tortilla sandwich that they must have made that morning. I'd always heard that Mex food was too hot for comfort, but in truth this stuff was all right.

"Slow now, boys," I reminded my crew, and Julio translated it into Spanish for the *vaqueros*.

"Another three miles," Julio told me. He smiled and reached into his saddlebags. He handed me a folded wad of papers. "With the compliments of our friend in Columbus."

The papers turned out to be a bill of sale and brand list for the herd, signed, or so it said, by an Arizona rancher named Victor Johnston. A fine American choice of a name, I noticed. There was also a very official looking certificate of brand inspection and another certifying that all the beeves had been vat dipped. Those two even carried embossed seals on them to prove their authenticity. I was impressed.

"If you guys don't watch out," I told Julio, "you're going to make me get awfully fond of you."

He grinned. "I did not know that you did not already feel so, my friend." He turned and began to lead his horse away.

"Wait."

He stopped and gave me a questioning look.

I took a couple steps closer and held out my hand to him. His smile when he took it reached deep into his eyes.

A half hour later he was dead.

CHAPTER 27

They hit us about a mile short of the border. Our Villista body-guard was riding in a loose screen around us as usual, but I think any halfway sensible ambusher would have deliberately done that, so I believe one of Julio's men must have ridden into them to start it.

Julio had been riding with Mrs. Lacey and me up near the point and on the right-hand side of our line of travel. With the first crackle of gunfire he began making arm signals to his men and dug the steel into his horse to head toward the action. He was about halfway to where I could see a few thin puffs of muzzle smoke when he took a hit that looked like he'd been slugged with a hammer. He pitched out of the saddle and face down onto the stony dirt. From the way he hit and bounced I was sure he was dead before he ever left his saddle.

The Villistas meanwhile were coming hard and returning the fire as they rode. I doubt they could have been doing much good by shooting from horseback like that, but they were making a hell of a lot of noise and anyone in front of them must surely have thought the air was full of bullets.

People always said how those Mex bandits were bullies and cowards and would run from any kind of a real fight. Not these boys. They couldn't have known how many men they were facing or how well armed, but they sure didn't back off any. They rode right into the teeth of whoever was up there.

I didn't have time to see any more than that. Those *corriente* steers spooked at all the noise and bolted to the west, away from it all.

That herd—and Mrs. Lacey—were my responsibility, so I

raked the rented horse I was on and kited off after the herd with Mrs. Lacey beside me. The crew and the *vaqueros* were doing the same.

"Don't turn 'em yet," I began hollering to the boys. "Let 'em run out a bit first."

This was a pretty decent crew, especially the *vaqueros,* and I figured they could have got the herd into a mill and stopped inside of a mile, and I just didn't want them stopped that close to the fight.

Behind us I could still hear shots, a lot of them now, and I didn't want the herd or Mrs. Lacey that close to the bullets.

We let them run, but they were pretty thin and in no decent condition for hard use after the kind of forage they'd been on, and after a couple miles they were noticeably slower. By three miles they were trotting and at four they were down to a walk and blowing hard, with ropes of drool streaming off their muzzles but their eyes no longer wild or rolling.

"Turn 'em in now, boys. Turn 'em." I waved my arm in a slow circle, and the Mex boys understood what I wanted just as good as the Americans did.

I stood in my stirrups and tried to see what was going on behind us, but of course it was pretty far away now and the air was thick with dust from the running cattle.

"Do you hear anything?"

I shook my head. "No, ma'am."

"Do you think it is over then?"

"I don't know much about such things, Miz Lacey, but I would think so. Short and hard, like. Not like that trench warfare stuff."

"And who . . . ?"

Again I had to shake my head. "I sure wish I knew, ma'am."

One of the riders moved in closer. "Do you want to let them bed, Cowboy?"

"Lord, no. If we let 'em get down now they might be hard to move again in a hurry. Come to think of it, Roy, we better shove them up to the border now. Just in case."

He nodded and reined away to tell the rest of them. He was right to have reminded me. It wouldn't be good for them to stop now until we were safely across onto U.S. soil. Then maybe we could let them lay up and rest awhile.

The crew got them pointed north. Behind us the dust was beginning to settle and I thought I could see some movement back there.

"Miz Lacey, I'd like you to ride around to the far side of the herd. If anything happens, I want you to run ahead of them for at least a mile and then angle off toward the border. If we get separated, I'll meet you at the hotel in Columbus."

She nodded and gave me no argument. She was maybe a little pale, but she seemed fully in control of herself in spite of everything. I had to admire her for that. At once she reined her horse away and gigged him into a brisk trot.

Me, I sat and waited and wished I had a machinegun handy instead of a dinky little pistol.

There were riders back there all right. Quite a lot of them.

I watched them come closer and soon I could see that they were not wearing uniforms anyway. By the time they were within a quarter mile I began to recognize some of their horses. They were Julio's men.

I will admit that I felt a whole lot better after that.

There were twenty-two of them where there had been twenty-six a while before. The one who approached me did not look any too pleased to have won the fight, and I suspected that he was resenting the reason for it. I didn't blame him for that.

The man's English was not good, practically nonexistent. At that it was a lot better than my Spanish.

"Julio," he said. "*Mort*." He made a short, chopping motion. "Juanito. *Mort*. Pablo, Francisco." With his hands he signed that they had been hurt. I guessed they were still alive anyway.

He was trying to tell me something more, but I couldn't figure it out. I shook my head and he looked as frustrated as I felt now too.

"Federales," he said. "No. No. Federales." He pointed at me and let his finger aim from my boots to my hat. "*Vaqueros. Gringo vaqueros.* Not cav-a-ry. Not Federale." He sought for the word and found it. "Cowboy." And he sure wasn't meaning my name.

"Do you mean back there? Doing all that shooting? Do you mean it was Americans you were fighting back there?"

He shook his head and shrugged eloquently.

One of the others nearby who seemed to have been listening shifted his horse a step closer and reached into a vest pocket. He pulled out some empty cartridge cases and handed them to me.

At first I couldn't figure what they were supposed to mean. They were perfectly ordinary empty shells.

I finally got bright enough to notice what kind of guns the Villistas were carrying. They were regular old 7mm Mausers like you could buy mail-order surplus for a few dollars apiece, the same as the Spaniards and the Mexes had been carrying for years.

These empties weren't from any U.S. troopers' guns either. I couldn't remember for sure what those boys in Columbus had been issued, but they should have been Springfield or Enfield .30-06s. There was a small chance some of our troops might still be carrying the old .30-40s like Colonel Roosevelt's crowd used in Cuba way back when.

But these in my hand were short, squat little .44-40 cases like so many saddle carbines shoot. These sure weren't from any military weapon.

For that matter, I remembered now that I had seen powder smoke when the shooting began. No government weapons had used black powder in twenty-five years; all of them were smokeless cartridges and so were the Villistas' guns. You could still buy black-powder loads for the old Winchesters and such but not for any modern fighting arm.

So it hadn't been either the Mex cavalry or our own that had just pulled that ambush.

And if *they* weren't the ones that were after us . . . who the hell was?

"Go now?" Julio's replacement asked.

It snapped me back to earth. The boys already had the herd lined out toward the border. "Yes," I told him. "We go now." I bumped my horse into a lope, the Mexicans following close behind. Mrs. Lacey had a right to know this right away.

CHAPTER 28

The border here was no great shakes for, of course, the rocks and the mesquite recognize no boundaries. Someone—maybe our troopers or maybe theirs—had driven a stake into the ground with a rag tied on top of it. The Villistas seemed surprised to see that much of a marker there. I noticed a couple of them pointing to it as we crossed.

The herd was being kept in pretty tight order, but even so it takes quite a while to move nearly 3,000 head of stock past a given point, so it was some time before all were across and Mrs. Lacey and I could begin to breathe easier. The Mex *vaqueros* stayed on their side of the line and from here on the beeves were ours to handle. The Villistas stayed with us, though.

We could have timed the crossing better. It was already past midafternoon and the steers, especially after their running, should be watered before they were bedded. I had no idea where water could be found hereabouts. What was more, I wanted to bed them north of the rails and did not know how far we would have to travel to accomplish that. If Julio had been with us I'm sure I could have asked him and gotten an answer on both counts, but of course he was not. I explained the problem to Mrs. Lacey.

"I will accept your judgment, Cowboy. Whatever you decide."

"In that case, ma'am, we'll just keep going north and turn back east when we cross the tracks. There's just as good a chance of finding water that way as any other, and I do want to get north of the railroad. Besides, that's the shortest way to Columbus and some leading pens."

She nodded. "That's good enough for me."

As it turned out I needn't have worried about it. We picked up a guide service of sorts. The United States cavalry, no less.

We were a mile or so north of the border and moving slow but steady when the Villista leader rode to me and began pointing north, in the direction dead ahead of us. His eyes or maybe one of his scouts' were pretty darn good for there was just the faintest hint of rising dust in that direction.

The man tried to explain something to me in Spanish, but I wasn't getting any of it. I shook my head.

With his hands he outlined for me a flat-brimmed, peaked little hat and a high collar with lots of buttons on the chest and bat-winged riding britches. That was clear enough where the words had not been. Those were Yankee troopers moving down toward us.

Lordy, but I could very happily have crawled under a rock and taken a week-long nap right then.

I looked at the Mex bandits and they were busy checking over their weapons. There just wasn't any way I could let them start shooting at our troopers.

"Did you understand what he was saying?" I asked Mrs. Lacey.

"Yes." She swallowed hard. She'd done just fine when that earlier fight was going on, but she was as pale as percale now. "We have to stop them," she said.

"Which them?"

"Either, I don't care which."

"If we just spoke Spanish we might could send these boys off and take our chances with the troopers. I've got those papers. We could say we'd drifted south of the border by mistake, looking for water or better grazing."

She nodded and shifted her horse around so she was on the other side of the Mex with him between the two of us. She pointed out toward where his men were riding and in a loud voice said, "English. Do . . . you . . . have . . . man . . . speak . . . English?"

He shook his head. "I speak."

She looked frustrated. Still almost shouting, though what good volume might do where comprehension didn't exist I could not know. She said, "No . . . fight. You no fight cavalry." She mimicked pointing a rifle north and then shook her head violently, "No fight. Wait." She pointed to me. "He talk. No fight. Meet you later."

The man said something, a considerable string of something, in Spanish and loped away toward his men. He began to wave them all in toward him.

I never will know, I guess, whether he understood Mrs. Lacey or if that was his own idea and he'd been trying to explain it to us. Either way, he gathered his men into a small group, gave us a wave and slipped out of sight into the scrub to the east. The Mexes were there and then they were gone, and they raised no dust to mark their passage.

Those boys had helped us an awful lot, but under the circumstances I was glad they were gone.

A while later the troopers came into view, and I was doubly glad the Villistas weren't around to oppose them. There were only a half dozen of them in the detachment, led by a sergeant who looked tough enough that you could strike matches on his jaw. *After* he shaved.

If it had come to a fight, though, those boys wouldn't have stood a chance against so many well-armed Mexes. I noticed as they came near that these fellows were carrying sidebox .30-40 Krags in their scabbards. There wasn't a lever action .44 among them.

The sergeant drew rein in front of me and gave Mrs. Lacey a fretful, sideways, glance. He threw me a smart salute and snapped out, "Begging your pardon, sir, but would you mind explaining your presence."

The lead steers reached where our horses were standing and began to flow around us like water around an island. The sergeant's eyes never left my face.

I gave the man a smile that I hoped did not look as phoney as it felt.

"Of course not, Sergeant." I reached into my saddlebags for the faked papers Julio had given me at noon. I tried to ignore the downward shift of the troopers' hands toward their weapons when I reached for the bag.

This was turning out to be an awfully long day.

CHAPTER 29

The sergeant read our papers without any change in the stoniness of his expression. Without turning his head he snapped out an order, "Fetler! Inform the lieutenant of our situation and request that he join us." A very formal man, our sergeant. *He* wasn't any World War conscript. This one had been around for a while.

One of the troopers barked out a fast "Yes, sir" and wheeled his horse around. He put the animal into a canter toward the northeast, riding in that straight-backed, rigid-looking way the Army seems to require.

"Are our documents not in order, Sergeant?" Mrs. Lacey asked. She wasn't a bad actress. I was guessing that she would be as nervous about this as I was, yet her voice was haughty if not completely cold. The implication was clear in her tone. How dare such an inferior person question her right to do whatever she did.

"They would appear to be, ma'am," the sergeant said formally.

"Then you will please stand aside."

"Begging the lady's pardon, but I cannot do that." In a sharper voice he said, "Trooper Marwell!"

"Sir." One of the troopers straightened to attention and moved his horse up beside the sergeant's. His head and eyes were locked straight ahead. He didn't give a look to Mrs. Lacey now although all the troopers had been giving her sideways glances before then.

"Trooper Marwell," the sergeant continued, "was on post immediately to the east. He reported hearing gunfire to the south and east of his position on the Mexican side of the boundary. He later observed dust and saw your passage from south to north of that line." Directly to me he asked, "Would you care to have your herd backtailed, sir? I believe their path should be clear enough."

I shrugged and tried to look unconcerned. "You may if you wish, Sergeant, and maybe you'll prove something if you do. Personally, I don't know just where the border is around here. If you say we crossed it, then most likely we did." I gave him a smile. A disarming one, I hoped. "We heard some shooting too and turned wide of it."

"Very good, sir." He sure didn't sound convinced of anything.

"Would you, uh, know where we might be able to water these cattle, Sergeant?"

"That will be up to the lieutenant, sir."

"Then I suggest we at least ride along with the herd until the lieutenant arrives, Sergeant," Mrs. Lacey put in. "In fact, I insist upon it. They are my stock and I will not be separated from them."

"Yes, ma'am," he said politely. It was pretty obvious he was not giving up a thing that was important to him and that he would not in the future, not for the lady or for anyone else.

We all began to move along with the herd and angled out beside it away from the worst of the dust. At least it didn't matter now that we were raising dust.

The sergeant rode in silence beside us, and the four troopers took up a two-by-two position immediately to our rear. There wasn't much to do now but wait.

The beeves had reached the railroad tracks and were crossing there when we saw another small detachment of troopers loping along the right of way. If we were going to be in for it, I guessed, now was when it would start. This time there was a guidon being carried with the crowd.

We reined to a stop beside the rails while the crew kept the cattle moving across. For a change, just for a moment there, I wished I was just another hand again instead of owning some of these animals. The troopers rattled to a smart stop near us and almost but not quite managed to keep their formation intact. This seemed to be a real by-the-book bunch of boys.

The lieutenant was as stoney-faced as his sergeant but a whole lot younger. He sat poker stiff and accepted a report—a fast, fair and complete one, I noticed—from the noncom. The sergeant also handed him the papers Julio or somebody had forged. The officer read them, cleared his throat and looked up very sternly.

The young fellow's composure slipped some then. His eyes widened and his mouth gaped open a bit. "Miss Turnbull?"

She inclined her head slightly and gave him a shy smile. "Lieutenant Schrunk." I hadn't recognized him myself.

Schrunk looked downright uncomfortable now, and he did seem to be in something of a box. It was pretty plain that this was a regular spit-and-polish outfit he was leading, and the ears if not all the eyes of his sergeant and nearly a dozen troopers were on him. Yet the person he was expected to question and maybe even arrest was the same young lady he had so recently been asking to dinner.

He did manage to get himself back together quickly, I do have to say that about him. He laid a hard look onto me and said, "Mr. Russel, isn't it?"

I nodded.

"Please be so good, sir, as to have your men halt the herd."

"I'm not so sure that's a good idea, Lieutenant. They're needing water, an' we don't know how far we'll have to go to find some."

He pondered that for just a scant second. "Very well. Drive them east along the railroad. There is a tank within two miles of here. Sergeant Perkins!"

"Sir." The sergeant sat even straighter.

"Have the men accompany the livestock, Perkins." Pointedly he added, "You will maintain a position to the *south* of the herd body, Sergeant."

"Yes, *sir*." Perkins gave him a snappy salute and delivered a rapid-fire series of commands. The lieutenant's detachment and the sergeant's formed into one and clattered away to the south of the tracks.

Me, I turned away to tell the boys to swing the herd and point them east. Mrs. Lacey and Schrunk were left sitting their horses alone behind me. Under the circumstances, I decided, that might be a very good thing.

Mrs. Lacey looked considerable shaken up. Oh, from a distance I'm sure none of the others could tell it. The crew wasn't likely to be paying attention anyway. They were too busy trying to move 2,850 head of steers past the couple measly watering troughs that had been put at one of the railroad's windmills and water tanks. They would be at that chore most of the night if not all of it, and already we were having to "borrow" water from the engine tank because the thirsty steers drank it faster than the wind pumped it.

The troopers, including Lieutenant Schrunk, were dismounted at ease on the south side of the tracks. One of the troopers was missing, I noticed.

Anyway, Mrs. Lacey was putting on a calm, serene front, but up close where I was sitting I could see the trembling in her underlip. It wasn't much, but it was there.

"If you don't mind me asking, ma'am . . . ?"

"What Lieutenant Schrunk said. Of course." She sighed. "He was very apologetic. And more than a little pretentious. Silly, if you ask me."

So much for dinners with Lieutenant Schrunk, I thought.

"He explained at great lengths about duty and honor," she went on. "He said it was beyond his powers of discretion to give us passage. He has to consult with his captain for a decision. Although of *course* if it were up to him alone we could go right ahead." She looked disgusted now. "So here we sit until this Captain Coursey arrives from Columbus."

"At least the cattle can water here. That had to be done anyhow, so it isn't like we're losing time. We wouldn't have moved till morning regardless."

She gave me a weak smile. "Thank you, Cowboy."

"Sure."

"Cowboy."

"Ma'am?"

"What do you . . . think our chances are? Truly?"

I grinned at her and shrugged. "I knew a fellow once. Came from Wyoming where he liked to hunt. He shot an elk once, laid his gun down to dress it out and the thing jumped up mad an' tried to hook him. There was a little bit of rock on the hillside there and one of them undercut to form a shallow hole. So he jumped into it where the elk couldn't get him. Soon as the elk turns away he pops back into plain sight. Mr. Elk sees him an' comes charging again. Back in the hole he goes. No sooner's the elk turned away than out he comes again. That goes on for the better part of half an hour until finally the elk drops from the wound that put him on the ground to start with. When he told people about it afterward they'd always ask, 'But, Bill, why didn't you just stay in that hole till the fool elk went off or laid down?' 'Boys,' he'd say, 'I likely would've but there was a damned ol' bear holed up in there first an' he was beginnin' to fret an' mutter some.'"

She gave me an odd sort of look, like maybe she thought I'd gone and flipped or something. "That is all very interesting, Cowboy, but . . ."

"Point is, ma'am, I heard that story from old Bill Cook's own mouth. He was in a bad situation there, but he was around a long time afterward to talk about it."

"Thank you, Cowboy." She smiled. "I think."

CHAPTER 30

It was well past dark and the boys were still watering cattle when the captain arrived amid a great racket of shod hooves and jangling equipment. If it was fair to judge by these guys, it was no wonder our cavalry had so much trouble with the Indians back in the old days. I think they'd been trained with the idea they would have to oppose an army of deaf men.

On the other hand, I don't know anything about the military so I am probably being unfair to them.

Captain Coursey turned out to be thirtyish, heavily moustachioed and otherwise completely unlike what I might have expected. He seemed a quiet, gentle sort of man, far from the pushy, overbearing sort I'd been waiting for. This one seemed a gentleman by more than act of Congress.

We heard the arrival of course, would have had to stuff our ears with cotton balls to not hear it, but it was a half hour or forty-five minutes before a corporal delivered the captain's compliments and begged our pardon and went through all the formal folderol that, boiled down, meant Mrs. Lacey and I were supposed to jump and run for our audience.

Mrs. Lacey handled it very well, I thought.

Here we were somewhere in a near-desert practically in the middle of the night, surrounded by soldiers and *corriente* cattle, saddle weary and dust caked. Moreover, we had been in this same spot for some hours now. Yet now was the time she chose to straighten her petticoats and completely repin her hair. Short as her hair was, of course, I couldn't see a bit of difference between first and last, but it was her right as a lady. The corporal stood patiently at attention the whole time.

"Very well," she said when she was quite ready.

"Yes, ma'am." The corporal led us across the tracks, not forgetting to offer Mrs. Lacey his arm so she could manage to step over each rail without sprawling.

Chuckling about the corporal being so darn formal, I tripped over the second rail myself and damn near fell down.

We passed a tidy row of tents that hadn't been there the last time I'd looked and came into sight of a larger tent that was showing a glow of lantern light from within. That was where we found the captain.

No wonder we'd had to wait awhile before we saw him. His camp cot was set up and the blankets stretched drum-tight. There were four canvas chairs set up and a cunning little field desk complete with ink well and papers. The captain and Lieutenant Schrunk stood when Mrs. Lacey entered.

"Thank you, Corporal." The captain's voice was soft. It sounded like he was really thanking the man instead of repeating something by rote. The corporal saluted, did a smart about-face and left.

We went through a round of politeness to get everyone seated and the captain said, "Now then, Miss Turnbull . . ."

"Please," she interrupted, "no false pretenses or misassumptions, Captain. Turnbull is my maiden name. I was married to a man named Lacey who deserted me. I am in the process of . . . seeking a divorce." Which was the first I knew of that and possibly the first time she did too. Lieutenant Schrunk had the grace to turn a bit pink at the news.

"That explains a question I had," Coursey said. He took some papers from his desk, looked at them briefly and nodded. When he held them up like that I could see they were the bill of sale and certificates I had given the sergeant earlier. They must have had Mrs. Lacey's name on them and perhaps mine too. I hadn't paid that close attention to them when Julio gave them to me. I had seen what they were and who they were made out *from*, but not *to*. It hadn't seemed important at the time.

The captain went on. "Tell me, Mrs. Lacey, do you deny that you crossed those cattle into the United States from Mexico?"

"I believe my foreman, Mr. Russel, answered that earlier, Captain. I neither affirm nor deny it. We were indeed south of the railroad. Other than that I couldn't tell you."

"According to our scout reports, sir . . ."

"I am already aware of the scout reports, Lieutenant. Thank you."

That was a rebuke sure enough, but Coursey's voice was still mild and gentle. The man wasn't a milktoaster anyway. I could see that it would be easy to think that he was and maybe then to underestimate him.

"We have reason to believe that these animals have been imported illegally, Mrs. Lacey," the captain said gently. "Our Government is doing its best to work cooperatively with the Government of Mexico. The export ban is theirs. And, of course, we do have health restrictions of our own."

"I would not know about your information, Captain. As for the laws of both countries, you have our papers." She was putting on a very cool front indeed.

"Mr. Russel?"

I shrugged. "There's not much I could add to what the lady's already said."

Captain Coursey nodded. He handed me the papers. "Lieutenant Schrunk, please escort Mrs. Lacey to her camp. She and her people are not to be detained."

"And the herd, sir?"

"Would you like me to put my orders in writing, Lieutenant?"

"No, sir," Schrunk said quickly. He snapped to attention and bowed. "Mrs. Lacey?"

"Thank you, Lieutenant. And you, Captain." She was very much the gracious lady as she made her exit.

We sat back down, alone now, and I looked the captain over some. "You wanted me to stay, I believe?"

He nodded. "I do."

"All right then." I leaned back against the canvas and waited for him to go ahead. It was his party.

"What name do you go by, Russel?"

"That's a strange question for a man to ask."

"I have a reason for it."

Like I said, it was his party. "Cowboy," I told him.

He nodded as if I'd told him a whole lot more. It seemed that I had. "There are a lot of rumors along this border," he told me. "Once in a while they even turn out to be true."

"Meaning?"

"One we heard a few days ago was that there was a married woman and a cowboy named Cowboy who stole some money from her husband, a rancher up north, and were planning to use it to buy Mexican cattle and slip them across the border illegally. But the husband learned about their scheme and was hiring a gun crew to get back what was his."

"Interesting," I told him.

"I thought so," he said. "But then most of these rumors turn out to be nothing at all."

"Uh-huh. Captain, could I ask a blunt question?"

"Go right ahead."

"What made up your mind for you?"

"Your papers are perfectly in order."

"Sure." I started to get up.

"Wait."

I settled back into the chair.

"Officially it is because your papers are in order, Russel. Also, I heard *another* rumor a while back about a man named Jack Lacey and a scam he pulled on an old ranching family. Schrunk tells me that the Turnbulls are an old ranching family."

"Very old," I agreed. "Very highly respected. But I can't believe that a family reputation would carry that much weight with you."

He gave me a thin smile. "Score one for you, Russel. That wasn't quite all of it. The . . . uh . . . party spreading this rumor made quite a point about the shady, immoral, indeed vulgar relationship between this married woman and her cowboy lover." He permitted himself a broader smile. "I don't think the facts fit the rumor very closely this time."

"No, I'd say they don't." I shifted forward on the chair again with the intention of leaving, but again he stopped me.

"Russel, there is another rumor that I've heard."

"Yes?"

"This one says that a man named C. K. Moberly was killed early this afternoon in Mexico, but that the rest of the gun crew hasn't given up."

So the Villistas hadn't been inaccurate in that scrap. "Like you said, Captain, you'll hear lots of rumors along this border."

"Yes, well, so much for small talk." He stood. "Will you be shipping your herd from Columbus, Russel?"

"I expect so."

"My command will be riding there in the morning. Slow field march. I think we will leave about six."

I grinned at him. "Maybe we'll run into you along the way."

"Quite possible," he said drily. He hadn't said a thing about an escort, but it looked like we would have one. "In case you are wondering, I like for this section of the border at least to be quiet. I really do like peace and quiet, you see."

"Yes, and . . . thank you for the small talk, Captain." I touched the brim of my hat to him and only realized afterward how close to a salute that was. "Good night."

"Good luck."

CHAPTER 31

I think that once I uttered the name Jack Lacey, Mrs. Lacey never understood another word I said. That had all of her attention.

"It has to be Jack behind that gunfight this afternoon. It has to be, Cowboy. And of course that makes perfect sense. He might well think we came down here after him. And he must know the plight of the Three-X. I would be far less of a threat to him penniless than if I should be able to recover. He knows, oh he *must* know how I hate him. Oh, Cowboy, I do hope he tries it again. I hope he comes against us again. I hope he does it in person this time. I hope I see him face to face, Cowboy. I'll kill him. I swear I will."

"That won't happen tomorrow anyway."

"Why not?"

"The Army escort, ma'am."

"Escort?"

I'd told her once already but she had not been listening. I told her again.

"We don't have to go with them. We could make a late start in the morning, give the cavalry a long lead before we begin. He might try it that way. He might feel safe enough."

"Ma'am, he might, if for sure it is him. Be safe enough too. No, ma'am. What we need to do tomorrow is get those steers to Columbus and get them safely sold and shipped. You can look for revenge with the money in your purse as easy as otherwise."

"All right," she said, temporarily subdued. "But, oh, isn't it a wonderful opportunity?"

"I don't know, ma'am. And neither do you. Go on to bed now. Tomorrow might be a long day."

Come morning we were ready to move in plenty of time and had to wait a little while for the soldier boys to finish breaking their camp. That was one delay I didn't mind at all.

And in spite of the late start we were at the loading pens on the edge of town by midafternoon. Columbus had been a lot closer than I'd figured.

Captain Coursey never so much as looked our way as the point riders started the herd into the yard. The troopers just happened to be passing at the same time, and civilian cattle were of no interest to them of course. I waved at him anyway.

I told the crew to stay with the beeves and took Mrs. Lacey straightaway to the telegraph office. I didn't know any commission men down here, but I figured that should be no problem.

A wire to Kansas City brought an answer within half an hour. They had a man in El Paso, and he would be on the westbound leaving there at 4:15. His name was Ferguson and he would meet us at the pens as soon as he got in. That would be in about an hour and a half.

"Do you want to wait at the hotel, ma'am?"

She shook her head. "I'm entirely too nervous to sit. Could we wait at the yard instead?"

"Whichever you'd rather."

She had had more than enough time in the saddle lately so we took the horses back to the livery, paid our bill there and walked the rest of the way to the pens.

The steers were comfortable enough there it seemed and were engaged in trying to double their weight by sopping up water. I wished them luck at it.

As was to be expected there was a goodly crowd of loafers and layabouts gathered at the rails, some of them jawing at our crew and some offering criticism on how poor these animals were. I couldn't help but wonder how many beeves each of that class owned.

Half or more of the loafers were Mexicans. I supposed that

was natural enough here, but something somehow seemed just a bit out of kilter. I studied on that some and finally it came to me. These Mex layabouts were dressed somewhat better than your average peon.

Once I got to paying that much attention to them I paid a little more, and pretty soon I had to smile some to myself. At least some of those Mexes were boys I lately had been riding with. It seemed we still had ourselves a bodyguard.

We chattered for a while about nothing important, Mrs. Lacey's excitement growing now more and more as she realized how near she was to chasing the wolf at least a better distance from her door.

Some of the other onlookers seemed to have been doing some early imbibing for they were loud but mostly merry. One fellow, obviously a town type, slipped off the rail he was sitting on and fell in with the steers. Those animals were too skittish and road-fogged to want to be anywhere near anything human, but he didn't know that. I'll bet all he could see of them was hooves and horns and not how they shied away from him. For sure he didn't wait around observing but went out under the bottom rail in a rapid crab-walk that left his clothes much to poorer in appearance and his buddies much the richer in merriment.

Not two minutes later there was another commotion on the far side of the pens but too far away for us to see. Everyone seemed to be in a fine humor this afternoon.

A moment or two afterward a couple boys from our crew rode over to us, and one named Roy leaned down to where he could talk without being heard too far.

"D'you notice that little fuss across the way?" he asked.

"I couldn't see what happened, but some drunk fell off the fence over here a bit ago."

"Well this wasn't no drunk," he said. "This was some hardcase with a big damn gun under his coat. One second he was standin' there lookin' around and slippin' his hand down near that gun. The next second there was a couple of those Mex bandits beside him. They took holt of him an' he turned plumb

white. Next thing you know they'd lifted his iron and were mar-
chin' him off somewhere. And I'd swear I recognize them as
being part of that crowd that was riding with us down south."

"That wasn't your imagination. I spotted a couple of them
too."

"The thing is, Cowboy, we been pretty patient with you an'
the lady, but we don't want any trouble between white men an'
Mexes an' us on the side of the Mexes, you know?"

"Those Mexes are protecting Mrs. Lacey, Roy. It isn't bandit
trouble if that's what is bothering you."

"I reckon it was, but I will take your word for it."

"You can pass that along to the others if you want. For that
matter, you signed on to help bring the herd here and you did it.
You can bow out now if you want to."

He seemed to be thinking that over. "Are you needing anything more from us?" he asked.

"I need the herd watched tonight at the least and the car-load-
ing done. Tomorrow if we can arrange it that soon."

Roy looked back at Bobby Greer who was with him. He got a
nod from Bobby and said, "Okay, we'll stick until the cars are
loaded. But we aren't gun hands an' you aren't paying gun
wages, Cowboy."

"I know that. I appreciate it, Roy, Bobby."

When they were out of earshot Mrs. Lacey eased closer to me.
"Are we in trouble, Cowboy?"

"I don't think so, ma'am." By golly I even managed to sound
jolly confident when I said it.

The truth was that I hadn't any idea but was thinking we probably were more than we weren't. There just wasn't any way to
know for sure.

Without making it real obvious what I was doing, I guided
Mrs. Lacey closer to where a group of familiar-looking Mexicans
were idling.

CHAPTER 32

Mr. Ferguson was a tall, slender built man verging on old age. He had the look of a man who knows his business, though, and wore his business suit in such a way that it matched his boots and hat as well as old jeans and a flannel shirt would have. I would have bet most anything I owned that this old man had gone up the grand old trails back when the country was free range and unfenced from border south to border north.

We made the introductions and Ferguson squinted at the fast-disappearing sun.

"I don't mean to be rude, folks," he said, "but we'd best look over these bovines while we have the light for it. Also before I forget to tell you, there's no scales here in Columbus, but we can weigh them up for you in El Paso or in K.C. No dockage for shrink loss if you want them weighed in Kansas City, of course."

"No rep watching the scales either, though, and if you weigh them in El Paso you'll charge us for the off-loading and railcar demurrage. No, Mr. Ferguson, I trust that you and me both can judge what this lot weighs. Close enough to it. And this is a downright uniform-sized herd, as you can also see with a naked eyeball. So I just think we'll sell by the head instead of the hundredweight," I told him.

What I said was true enough but the fact is that it was more excuse than reason. If they sold by weight it would be some time —maybe several weeks if they were weighed out in Missouri— before any money changed hands. Going by the head they could be counted in the morning and a check written out on the spot. Now *that* was the way we wanted it.

"If you'd rather," Ferguson said mildly. He tipped his hat to Mrs. Lacey and said, "Excuse us, ma'am?"

She smiled and nodded, and Ferguson slipped between the pen rails and inside. I followed him in among the steers.

Now I've known some commission men and yard buyers who could put on an act of studious appraisal that would shame a ham actor every time they looked at a cow, and I've seen others who got so serious about it you'd have thought they were performing a religious rite or something. Ferguson was good enough that he didn't need to put on a show for the sellers. He just kind of wandered through the bunch and offered an occasional comment on the weather, the grass and the National League pennant race. When he'd seen enough he said, "Pretty uniform, I agree. I'd judge the average around 520."

"I'd have said 525 per head."

"I think we're close enough we don't have to argue."

"I agree, Mr. Ferguson."

He never said another word of business until we were back with Mrs. Lacey. I was glad to see there that she hadn't been as alone as she looked. There were three Mexicans loafing nearby.

"Do you want me to list all the pluses and minuses for you, Mrs. Lacey?"

"A final figure might do, Mr. Ferguson." She smiled. "Without an explanation about the depressed state of the beef market. My father always told me to be wary of buyers who insist on making excuses for their own industry."

His laughter was deep and, I believe, sincere. "I know the type your daddy meant, Mrs. Lacey. Believe me, I had no intention of offering you excuses. What I am offering is six and a half cents a pound on a per-head basis, or $33.80 each."

I think Mrs. Lacey was willing to scream and shout and jump for joy right there and then. I jumped in with, "Thirty-four fifty sounds better to me."

Patiently he explained, "My employers already instructed me to go as high as decent business sense would allow." He smiled. "Your father always conducted his business in Chicago, Mrs.

Lacey. In the future we would like an opportunity to participate in the Whiskey's business."

"That is very kind of you, Mr. Ferguson. Particularly since you are assuming there will be future business from the Three-X," she said.

"You certainly have the spirit to make a success of yourself, ma'am." His lingering smile turned into a grin. "I don't claim to know the entire Arizona brand book, Mrs. Lacey, but I do know most of the brands in that country. And a good many south of the border too."

"Mm, yes."

"We'll accept $33.80 a head, Mr. Ferguson."

"Good." He extended his hand and the deal was as firm as any contract could have made it. "I'll go order the cars now. With any luck they can be dropped on the siding some time tonight and we can load tomorrow."

Ferguson hadn't much more than gotten out of sight before a Mexican, one I hadn't seen before, was at my elbow.

"Señor Alvarez would like to see you. Would you an' the lady please follow, yes?"

"Miz Lacey?"

"All right."

We followed. There were an awful lot of Mexes about now. Enough to stage a second invasion of Columbus, I thought.

He took us into a saddler's shop and straight on through it into the alley behind. There were some more Mexicans in the alley, three of them leaned up against a wall with an uncorked bottle. Every one of them looked sober, though, and while they were flashing their jug they weren't doing any drinking from it. We turned right and climbed a set of back-wall stairs two buildings on. Alvarez and several other well-dressed men were waiting for us.

"I am sorry I am doing business with you," Alvarez said without preamble. And without rising. "It becomes very troublesome."

"Julio was a good man," I told him. Mrs. Lacey, I think, didn't know quite what to say. "I don't wonder that you regret losing him and your other man as well. We didn't know either that it would be like this."

Alvarez nodded. "The troopers we can deal with. These gringo bandits . . . Pah!" He added some words in Spanish that I was just as glad I couldn't understand and hoped Mrs. Lacey didn't either.

"Who are they?" Mrs. Lacey asked.

Alvarez shrugged. "Hired men. People of no consequence."

"The man who hired them . . . ?"

"A large man going under the name Jones hired them. His name was not Jones. His cigar case and his luggage had on them the letter L."

Mrs. Lacey paled. We were still standing and she began to sway a bit so that I took her elbow to steady her. I don't think she noticed. "Could the man have been Jack Lacey?"

"I would not know, Señora. In truth, I would not care. I want now only to go with you to the bank and receive my money as was agreed. That is why I speak with you now. The bank is to open at nine. You will meet me there?"

"Of course," she said.

"If not at nine then as close to it as we can," I corrected. "We'll be loading cattle in the morning. We have to be there for the count. And I guess I'll be standing guard on them over at the pens tonight." I wanted to get that part in to make darn sure they'd know I was going to be there. I'd stay with the cattle and hope some of them would stay with me. After all, I had to show up at the bank in the morning too.

Alvarez must have gotten the message about having to protect the both of us through the night. He looked unhappier after that anyway. He muttered a few polite good wishes and reminded us again that he would see us at the bank in the morning. A couple minutes later we were back on the street.

CHAPTER 33

Oddly enough no one came near the beeves that night except me and a couple Mexican loafers. Or Mexicans pretending they were loafing. I was more than half expecting someone to try to mess with our steers, but nobody did.

The only thing at all that happened during the night was around 4:30 in the morning when a westbound short freight dropped a string of cars and one engine on the siding. Those, I figured, would be the ones Ferguson said he was ordering.

Anyway there was no attempt to turn the herd loose or to poison them or anything like that.

The first of the crew showed up around daybreak so I turned the guard detail over to the two of them and walked back to the hotel to collect Mrs. Lacey for breakfast.

She was already dressed and was down in the hotel restaurant when I came in. Mr. Ferguson was at the table with her so I joined them, feeling grimy and unshaven but wanting to get this over with.

"I think we can start any time you folks like," Ferguson said once he had pushed his plate away and tossed his napkin onto the table. He had eaten a hearty breakfast and after all night by the pens so had I, but Mrs. Lacey had just picked at hers. I was betting she was thinking about that Jack Lacey. Me, I was remembering that the initial L would fit for Lonahan as easily as it would for Lacey.

We went together to the loading chutes, and Ferguson had the first car drawn into position. They had kept the steam up during the several hours since they pulled onto the siding. The crew pushing the steers up the ramp, and Ferguson, Mrs. Lacey and I each began keeping a tally.

When all the loading was done I thought I'd miscounted somehow. My tally showed 2,912 head though we'd bought only 2,850. Ferguson's and Mrs. Lacey's showed exactly the same.

"That's a little over what we agreed to," I said. "Do you want to pull the extras off?"

"Of course not," Ferguson said. "Give me just a moment here."

He flipped to a fresh page in his notepad and did a little figuring. "Mm, at $33.80 I believe I owe you right at"—he finished his figuring and jabbed the pad with his pencil for emphasis—"$98,425.60."

I thought Mrs. Lacey was going to faint.

Just to make sure I took my own pencil stub and got the same figure. I made another calculation and said, "A hundred fifty of those are mine, so if my figures are correct I get $5,070 and the lady gets the rest."

Ferguson licked his pencil and checked my multiplication. When he was done he nodded. He checked a fat old Horologe in his pocket and said, "The bank's open, folks. Shall we?"

Ten minutes later Mrs. Lacey and I were each in possession of a certified check and Ferguson was properly thanked, handshaked and on his way. If anything happened to those beeves now it was the problem of Goodwin, Mulaub and Hanson Cattle Company. Mrs. Lacey still looked faint.

Five minutes more and Alvarez had his valise. He was about to leave, a bit rudely if understandably so, when Mrs. Lacey said, "Wait please."

"Yes?"

"There were more steers than there should have been."

Alvarez shrugged. "The Federales. I am told there was much confusion with them, with the animals. It is a thing that can happen."

"I want to pay you for them. I did some adding and subtracting." She dug into her purse and handed him another stack of the bright yellow coins. "I don't want to cheat you."

He looked at the money and then at her. He gave her a smile. It was a small one but it was a smile. "You are a nice lady. But please do not ask me to do business with you again."

"No. And I am sorry."

Alvarez said something in Spanish. It sounded like it must have been something very gallant. He tipped his hat and left. This time all of the bodyguards went with him.

"Let's pay off the crew, ma'am, and get the hell out of here."

"Wha . . . oh. Yes. Please. Please, Cowboy. Take me home."

She was crying a little as we left the bank. It was, I thought, a mixture of relief and disbelief. She had the money now to give her a chance—not a certainty but a darn good chance—to keep the Whiskey afloat.

CHAPTER 34

"It's over, Cowboy. It is really, finally over. I'm just now beginning to believe that." She dug into her handbag and once again pulled out the certified check Ferguson had given her. She had done that about every two minutes since we left Columbus, and now the conductor was announcing El Paso.

"Don't call it over," I reminded her. "That money gives you breathing room, but it won't put you home free. It'll take you several years, maybe a good many years, of sound management to get you completely clear again. It will take even longer to get you back to where your daddy was."

She sighed. "I know that. But even so, the bad part of it is behind me now. *This* time if anything goes wrong, it will be because of my decisions and not his."

I decided against reminding her that it was Jack Lacey who had put her behind the eight-ball and into a position where she could fail if she wasn't careful. She had had enough of a time of self-pity. This attitude was a whole lot better for her. For the Whiskey too, more than likely.

"I have been thinking about something, Cowboy," she announced a moment later.

The tempo of the wheels hitting the rail joints changed, and I could hear the squeal of brakes being applied. The outlying shacks and small houses of El Paso were flashing past the window.

"On those extra cattle," she said, "I want you to take half the profit."

I started to shake my head.

"No, Cowboy, I really will not take no for an answer about

this. I've already thought it over. Thanks to you I made enough and more than enough on the 2,700 head to do what has to be done. You are certainly entitled to half the profit on the rest."

"But, Miz Lacey, that would be nearly a thousand dollars."

"A thousand would do for a nice round number. Call it a bonus if you like. Just take it. There is another thing too."

The train came to a hissing, clanging stop, and I gathered our bags together. It was awfully nice to be traveling now without that heavy valise full of gold coin.

Mrs. Lacey led the way to the platform and resumed talking as if there had been no interruption. "I definitely will be needing sound management if I expect to succeed in the future. Your judgment has been invaluable to me during this crisis, Cowboy. I would like you to accept the position of foreman."

"That's very kind of you, ma' . . ." We were interrupted by a burly redcap who started off by stepping in front of us with a bow and a grin and the next thing was unloading me and loading everything onto himself. Neither of us had signaled for help, but he sure seemed anxious for the business.

"He'p you to a taxi, missus? mistah? Take you to a *ho*-tel? Need directions or advice? Whatever you need I can he'p." He was smiling and bobbing his head.

"We do need a cab," Mrs. Lacey said. We had to transfer to the D&RG terminal.

"Yes'm. Raht now." He hurried away so fast in spite of his load that we had to hustle to keep up. He headed around the side of the S.P. depot instead of into it and through to the cab stand. "'Void the crowd this heah way," he called over his shoulder.

Sure enough there was no crowd around there, just an unpaved parking area with some loafers idling in the shade.

The redcap set our bags down and shoved two fingers into his mouth. His whistle had a taxi around the corner and waiting by the time Mrs. Lacey and I caught up with him.

"That certainly was good service," Mrs. Lacey smiled. She groped in her handbag but I beat her to it and had tipped the fellow a quarter before she got her coin purse out.

"Thank you, missus, suh." He took his hat off and bobbed his head and loaded our bags into the front seat and told the driver, "You take good care o' these nice people, Barney. 'Deed you should."

Barney promised that he would. He handed Mrs. Lacey up into the back seat and waited while I crawled in beside her. He shut the door behind me and conscientiously checked to make sure it was latched tight. He went around and climbed in behind the wheel and ground maybe a half pound of metal off the gears getting into first gear. "Here we go now." He lurched into motion as if he hadn't much experience driving.

We motored along a paved road for a little piece and then turned north across the S.P. tracks and the driver built up speed. Within a couple minutes we were in the dry, thorny scrub. I leaned forward.

"Where are we, Barney?"

"Aw, a damn ol' culvert collapsed on the main drag in town. This's the easiest way around."

I looked at Mrs. Lacey.

She was no help. She held her hands palm up and said, "Don't ask me. I would recognize the way to the Paso del Norte or from there to the terminal. I never went from one station direct to the other."

"I know, but . . ." It just didn't *feel* right. I mean, I have made my way horseback across an awful lot of country without ever owning a map of any sort. I realize things are different in towns where the country is cut up into little squares and you have to go one way to wind up in another direction completely. But I never heard that city limit lines changed the points of the compass and I was just sure we were already too far north for the D&RG terminal.

"Hey, mister."

The driver looked around briefly. "It's okay, buddy. I know where I'm going."

"It's all right, Cowboy. He knows the town; we don't."

"Ma'am, we ain't *in* the town anymore."

There was something else that was bothering me too. Something else wrong.

"Good Lord, Miz Lacey," I hissed under my breath. "We never told this fellow where we wanted to go. An' he never asked."

It was a fine time for me to be thinking about that. Already way too late. The driver swung the wheel and we bounced into a rutted lane, across a cattle guard and back into a tangle of mesquite and black chaparral.

The cab shuddered to a halt and I made a grab for Barney's shoulder. He twisted away from me and tumbled out the door.

I guess I must have been confused for I sure didn't do anything constructive. I sat dumbly and watched him run away and out of sight around a particularly thick patch of brush.

A few seconds later I could hear a motorcycle engine starting up, and the machine roared away. Judging from the sounds it was heading back toward the road.

"Oh, Cowboy." Mrs. Lacey's voice was very small. I noticed that she had a hard grip on my left wrist. It might have been there for some time now. Certainly I hadn't noticed when she took hold of me.

"I think, ma'am, we might best get out of this car and find a place where we can't be seen so easy."

It was already too late for that too. Before I could reach the door handle a man stepped into view from behind the brush where we'd last seen Barney.

He was a big man and I was mortally certain that he would be carrying a cigar case with an L monogram on it.

The man's name was Lonahan.

CHAPTER 35

Lonahan.

All the stories, all the rumors, all the things I had heard about Henry Lonahan came flooding back to me. With them came fear.

"Who . . . ?"

I told her, and she seemed to shrink into the soiled cushions in the back seat of the car.

I tried to lick my lips but my tongue was as dry as they were.

Lonahan came out of the brush. He was carrying a shotgun, one of those boxy-looking automatic Brownings that shoots every time you pull the trigger. The barrel was cut down flush with the magazine, and I knew enough to know that it was one hell of a weapon.

I wondered what size shot he had loaded in it. That was, I know, a stupid thing to be thinking about. We were the both of us facing dying and what I was thinking about was not the dying but the tool that might be used to cause it.

He came closer and broke out into a smile. A couple yards short of the car he stopped. The shotgun dangled loose in his right hand. With his left hand he tipped his skimmer onto the back of his head, and he grinned at us.

"The way it worked out," he said, "I'm kinda glad. Those two-for-a-nickel idiots over in New Mexico might have got you, and then I would've missed out on this, you know? Terrible."

He paused and waited. I think he wanted us to say something, ask something. When neither of us did he went on.

"Reason I'm here, of course, is that the little lady there is in the way of the profits we figure to make directly she goes under.

But, Mr. Russel, having you tied up in this, that's just like getting a Christmas bonus in July." He chuckled.

"Somehow, Russel, I've always had it in mind that you're the sorry coward that jumped me from behind that night up in Colorado. You wouldn't want to tell me about that, I don't suppose."

He was right. That wasn't the kind of confession I wanted to make right now.

"No, I didn't think you'd have guts enough to admit it," he said.

Guts had nothing to do with it. Opening my mouth to him would have been suicidal and therefore double-stupid, and I'm not at all ashamed of myself for keeping my mouth shut and letting him talk.

"You and me would have talked about this before now, Russel, except for Mr. Tyler wanting to keep peace with your rich buddy. But now . . . we got plenty of time to talk now. I might just decide to get you to tell me all about it, Russel." He gave me a smirk and a wink. "An' I might decide to tell you all about that little gal up there you were so fond of. She turned out to be a regular little wildcat, you know? Built too. But then you already know about that, don't you?"

He cocked his head to the side and peered closer at Mrs. Lacey. "You now, lady, you aren't built that swell from what I've seen so far. Course your boyfriend here could probably tell me, couldn't he?" He laughed and it came out a very ugly sound.

"Maybe what I should do is get rid of him first and keep you around for a couple hours. See what kind of a workout you can give me."

Lonahan moved a step closer and shifted the shotgun in his grip. The son-of-a-bitch looked completely relaxed and happy.

"Do you know what Mr. Tyler told me, lady? He told me you are a real, genuine, old-family heiress and a lady. He said a couple years ago you were a debutante. Did I say that right? Yeah, I'm sure I did. I remember from when he told me about you. I never had a debutante before.

"Course that was before you got married. That kind of dulls

the edge a little but not too bad. You really were a debutante a couple years ago and that counts for something."

I glanced at Mrs. Lacey. Her jaw was set and her lips were drawn tight into a straight, thin line. She'd been scared before, but now she was beginning to get mad. I reached my left hand over and took both her hands in mine to try to comfort and ease her. From where he stood the driver's seat of the car kept Lonahan from seeing the movement. I didn't want to set him off.

"Yes, I definitely think that would be the best," Lonahan said. "Take care of the sneaky boyfriend there and then let you take care of me." He grinned. "If you're good enough, I might even let you live, you know? That's not a promise now. Don't think it is. But it is a possibility. I want you to think about that."

I licked my lips. The shock had worn off now. My mouth wasn't dry any longer. My breathing and my heartbeat were almost normal again. I cleared my throat.

"You like to play at being a tough Irishman, Lonahan." My voice was level. I had kind of wondered if it would be. "My people now, they were English 'way back when. Do you think one tough Irishman can lick one Tommy?"

"What?"

"It is simple enough. If I can whip you—and you can believe I'll try—I'll truss you up like a calf ready for branding and Mrs. Lacey an' I will run like mad. Otherwise," I shrugged, "I guess it won't matter." I laughed a bit, and oddly enough I didn't have to fake it. "Anyway I'd like a chance to land one on you."

Lonahan grinned and shook his head. "William S. Hart to the rescue, eh? Broncho Billy in action. You wouldn't have half a chance."

"I'll take what chance I can get."

"You must think I'm some kind of a fool," he said.

But he laid the shotgun down on the ground. He bent over and placed it carefully on the dirt. I noticed when he did it he took up a hidden palmful of sand, no doubt with the intention of throwing it in my eyes.

I sighed. He had wanted to work me over anyway. He had said as much a minute earlier.

But it was that shotgun being on the ground that I wanted. It was what I'd been waiting and hoping for.

Lonahan was grinning in anticipation.

I slid the muzzle of Mr. Abelard's big .45 across the top of the seat and began squeezing the trigger and I didn't stop until the gun was empty and locked open and the trigger wouldn't move anymore.

Mrs. Lacey had the side door open and was throwing up on the ground. She regained control of herself and used a handkerchief to dab at her mouth.

I wanted to speak to her but I knew her ears would be ringing as bad as mine were. The sound of a .45 automatic being fired under a metal car roof is something awful.

Mrs. Lacey got out of the car. She was moving slowly and kind of jerky, like a wooden puppet with wire where the strings should be.

Very carefully she walked over to where Lonahan lay. She examined him but she didn't trust him to be dead and the threat of him ended. I knew what she was feeling. I was feeling it too.

Very slowly, very deliberately she reached into her handbag and pulled out her little .32 revolver. Very carefully she positioned the muzzle behind Lonahan's ear and pulled the trigger. Just once. Just to be very sure. Only then did she return to the car.

"Ma'am? I hope you feel up to driving this car, ma'am. I don't know how."

She nodded and sat limply on the running board. "In a minute," she said. "Just give me a minute."

CHAPTER 36

The redcap backed away from the look I gave him as if I'd hit him instead of just looked at him. He couldn't know that I was thinking about another redcap far to the south, but I couldn't forget either.

It didn't matter. This was not a very big depot and it wasn't far to where we had left the Dort. I took her Gladstone bag under my left arm and carried my own war bag in my left hand. For the past day and a half I hadn't wanted my right hand occupied, and that bothered me. I was still the same person as always and yet I wasn't, and that bothered me too. Somehow, I thought, I should have been a whole lot different. I shouldn't be allowed to go on being the same person as always. Not now. Not after I killed a man. If it didn't affect me more than this, maybe I'd been no better than Lonahan to start with. I sighed and tried to quit thinking so damn much.

The Dort was hard to start, but eventually the engine caught and Mrs. Lacey nursed it into a smooth roar. My cranking arm and I were glad.

"Ma'am?"

She gave me a silent, questioning look. We hadn't spoken much to each other lately.

"I know you'll be anxious to get home, Miz Lacey, but would you mind taking me up to Monument on your way?"

She shook her head. I wasn't sure if she meant that she wouldn't mind or that she wouldn't do it. It was all right if she wouldn't. I could ride in if she didn't want to. The old horse would need some work after all this layoff anyhow.

We reached the county road turnoff that led east toward the Whiskey but she kept on north toward the town.

"I can find a way out to the place," I told her when she pulled to a stop in the town center.

"I'll wait." She cut the engine and stayed sitting there behind the wheel.

"I won't be long."

The cafe was fairly busy but the fellow I wanted to see wasn't among the customers. I looked at the two waitresses briefly. I recognized both of them, but the one I really would have liked to see there was long gone and likely would not be back. I wished I knew where she had gone. And to what. She might have liked to know about the man who had given her so much grief.

The stores where people tended to loaf didn't turn up anything and neither did the speakeasy where I was known.

The other speak wasn't far, though, and I had no trouble getting into it. It was for sure no one around here was worried about Volstead agents.

This place was just two rooms but fairly large ones. It was a much rowdier joint than the other one, more of a working man's hangout. Maybe I should have felt more at home here than in the other place, but drunks are only amusing if you happen to be drunk yourself. A sober man generally finds them barely tolerable, and I was certainly sober at the moment.

The front room was full of drunks and men on their way to being drunk, and I didn't know any of them. I pushed my way into the second room.

He was there, sitting at a table with a couple hale-fellows at his elbows and a pitcher of beer on the table before him. I went to him.

"Excuse me," I said to the man who was sitting between me and him. "Would you move back, please? Thanks." I smiled at him, but from his expression I would guess that it didn't come across very friendly. "It's good to see you, Mr. Tyler," I said.

Tyler looked every bit as shocked and as scared as Mrs. Lacey had looked when Lonahan stepped out from behind that chaparral down in Texas.

"I'd like to talk to you, Mr. Tyler. Outside."

He shook his head mutely.

"Oh, I think I will, Mr. Tyler. Now."

He swallowed hard but made no move to get up.

Tyler's hands were gripping the arms of the chair he was sitting in. I kicked the nearer one and caught his fingers between the wood of the chair and the sole of my boot. It probably broke them; it certainly bloodied them. Tyler's tablemates were companions but not friends. One of them gagged and both moved quickly out of the way.

"Now, Mr. Tyler."

The pain drew his face into a witch-mask but he still didn't say anything. Shakily he stood and walked toward the doorway.

I took him around behind the building. There was no one in sight.

Tyler slumped down to a sitting position on a discarded keg lying in the weeds there. He looked tired and quite old like that. He put his injured hand in his lap, ignoring the blood that dripped off his fingers onto his pants. I don't know if he was even aware of it.

"Your bulldog is dead, Mr. Tyler. I killed him myself."

He didn't react. He didn't raise his eyes or try to look beyond his own shoe tips.

I pulled the .45 from under my coat and let him hear me click the safety off. The gun was already cocked and had a cartridge in the chamber.

Tyler still wouldn't look up but he began to tremble. The shaking got worse until I could actually hear his teeth chattering together.

I laid the muzzle of the .45 behind Tyler's ear, in exactly the same place Mrs. Lacey had shot Lonahan to assure herself that he was gone.

For two days and a thousand miles I had looked forward to killing this man. I had thought of very little else during that long train ride. I had visualized all the many ways I thought it might happen including this one, and there was absolutely no doubt in my mind that I could and I would pull the trigger on him. Two killings would not be worse than one.

I couldn't pull the trigger.

Now that I was here, now that I was looking at him and seeing the sheeplike acceptance as he waited to die, I didn't even want to kill him anymore.

I didn't hate him, I realized. He disgusted me, yes, but the disgust was a less active thing than the hate had been.

I pushed the gun a little harder against his head.

"Mr. Tyler," I said softly, "I want you to leave Mrs. Lacey alone now. If she should manage to go broke again, you'd best not even think about buying Whiskey land. You'd best remember to not take any of it for free if somebody tries to force it on you. Because if you do, I'll take this here gun and put it just where it is right now and I'll blow your head apart like a ripe tomato.

"You're going to leave Monument now, Mr. Tyler. You aren't even going to stop to collect your car or your things. What you are going to do is walk over to those railroad tracks and start hiking toward Denver. Because if you don't do exactly that, I am going to kill you right here and now. You understand that?"

He nodded.

He obviously believed me even if I didn't. I took the gun away from his head and he stood up. He began to stumble and then run toward the tracks and toward Denver. He still hadn't looked at me.

And me, I felt drained now. The bucket had come empty somewhere in there.

I didn't feel proud of myself or of what I had just done. But at least I had learned something from it. I hadn't killed him. More, I hadn't wanted to. I was glad of that.

I put the safety back on the .45 and put the thing away out of sight. I sighed and began to walk back toward the car. Mrs. Lacey would be waiting for me.

CHAPTER 37

I gave her a few days to settle down while I rode the heifer pasture for her.

Lord, but it was good to be back to horse sweat and open sky and the sight of nursing calves again. I don't know how Mrs. Lacey's thoughts were running but that time of lazy pasture riding did more to put my nerves back together than a week-long blowout in Denver could have done.

The stock was in good enough condition. Most of the bred heifers had calved by now. While we'd been south there had been some losses. Not too awful many but enough to delight the coyotes, which were thicker in that particular area than I had seen them before.

I suppose I should have gotten busy with a rifle and poison baits, but I just wasn't in a mood for that. And anyway the calving was mostly over now, and coyotes mostly live on mice and jackrabbits. I figured I wasn't being disloyal by ignoring them now.

The fifth morning after we got back I showed up for breakfast at the usual time. Mrs. Lacey nodded a good morning; we still weren't talking a lot. She set out a platter of ham steaks and a pile of hot biscuits and ham gravy and a peach pie, and I loaded up heavy on all of it.

"The heifers are in good shape now, ma'am, but there's only so much grass in that pasture. I would say they should be moved out to the range grass in another two weeks. I marked that down on a slip of paper." I reached into my shirt pocket and laid the paper down.

"I marked down a few other things while I was at it. There's a contract haying crew coming in within a week or so. I ran into their advance man yesterday and told him to come see you. Personally, I think you should use them. Don't pay them the cash rate, though. As few animals as you're running you can hire them on shares. They can sell their part of it easy enough, and you won't be out any hard money. But make sure they agree to fence your stacks and fill the barn with loose hay. They'll likely try to overlook that little point an' save themselves some time. Don't let them get away with it. And check up on them later to make sure they actually do it like they agree to.

"The ranch horses are up in the corral. I'll turn all but one of them out in the trap, but you'll have to see to his feeding. Unless you want him turned out too.

"There's more fence repairs needed and someone really ought to be riding bog now, so it probably would be a good idea for me to find a boy and send him out to you. I should be able to find a youngster who'd work cheap for the chance at a riding job. One like that will stir the cattle up practicing his roping, but you don't have market beef on the place to worry about right now so I think he'd save you a lot more than he might cost you. I'll screen one out for you that I think knows enough to do the job you're needing."

"It sounds like you won't be here for a while," she said.

"That's right, ma'am. I packed my gear this morning."

"How long will you be away?"

"Well," I felt somewhat embarrassed by the directness of her question, "I guess I won't be coming back, ma'am."

"I thought . . . you were going to stay as my foreman." That was what she said. And it was a natural enough thing, of course, her having made the offer and all. But I thought sure that I could see relief in her eyes. There was none in her voice. She was too much a lady for that. I sure did think she looked relieved, though.

"I . . . uh . . . remember that you made the offer, and I do thank you, Miz Lacey. It is a high compliment and I take it as such.

"If you'll remember back, though, we were interrupted about then, and I never had a chance to give you my answer. Afterward . . . well . . . it just didn't seem important then.

"Anyway, I do thank you and I did give it a lot of thought. But, ma'am, I want more out of life than to ride over someone else's ground and to mark someone else's calves. The thing that brought me here was the idea of finding cheap land. The Whiskey's all right now—or it will be if you're careful and go about things the way your granddaddy would have—so I think the thing for me to do is to go somewhere else to look. I hope you understand that."

"Of course." She didn't go off into any false song-and-dance about wanting me to stay. After all that had happened, she would be as glad to get shut of me as I would be to get gone.

That was a shame in a way, but not much of one.

"Do I owe you anything now?" She blushed. "Wages, I mean. I owe you a great deal. I am not unaware of that."

"No, ma'am, you don't." Yesterday she had given me a check for half the profit on those excess steers, and I had made a tidy amount myself on the *corrientes* I had bought. For her to have handed me a couple dollars in day wages now would have been as awkward for me as it would have been for her.

"I don't know how to tell you . . ." she started.

"Don't then. It isn't needful." I smiled at her. "We can just consider it all said."

She smiled back at me. "Thank you."

We left the table and I got my hat and put it on. Mrs. Lacey hesitated. After just a split second, too little for her to think I had caught it, she extended her hand for me to shake. No friendly peck on the cheek there. Not for the hired help. The gulf was just too deep. I was glad I was going.

We shook hands and I turned away and caught up my old bay gelding in time to ride toward the mountains with the new sun coming up over my shoulder.

CHAPTER 38

I tied the bay to a tree on somebody's vacant lot, but there was plenty of room where I could have put him instead. The word seemed to be getting out, for Monument sure wasn't half as busy as the other times I had seen it and I guessed that it would be staying slack now. The speculators and the confidence men would be pulling out.

Mr. Abelard, I hoped, was not yet gone.

I knocked on his door and a moment later heard footsteps. "Curtis?"

It was a woman who opened the door, though. A lady I'd never seen before. "I'm looking for Mr. Abelard."

She gave me a hard looking over and found a dust-covered cowboy instead of a gentleman business caller. "He ain't here."

"Is he still in town? I need to see him."

"I told you, he ain't here."

"Could I leave a message then? My name is Russel and . . ."

"*You?*" She sounded downright disbelieving. I don't know what kind of comments she might have been hearing at the dinner table, but whatever they were she'd heard the name but sure hadn't made the connection. She swung the door wider.

"Mr. Abelard, he's taking his lunch over to the cafe, Mr. Russel. If you wanta wait I'll fetch him for you." That sure was a different tune she was playing now.

"No, ma'am. I thank you, but I can just go over there myself." I tipped my hat to the snobby old bat and left.

The place was all but empty now. Two customers sitting at a table near the front and Mr. Abelard alone at a table to the rear and that was all there was. The place was down to a single waitress too and she looked mighty well rested.

Curtis saw me come in. He hopped to his feet and met me halfway across the room with one hand held out to shake and the other up and onto my shoulder to squeeze. "Cowboy! I've been worried about you." He gave me a friendly shaking. "It's good to see you."

We were both doing plenty of grinning and stamping the way friends will do, and I discovered that I was as tickled to see him as he seemed to be to see me.

"Bring another cup of coffee," he told the waitress, "and whatever my friend wants for his lunch. And keep the coffee coming, missy, we have a lot of catching up to do."

We sat and talked and drank coffee and let our food get cold, and I told him most if not quite all of what had happened.

"You won't be staying on at the Triple-X then?" he asked, leaning back in his chair and looking, I thought, a bit smug.

"No, I've got all my gear out on my horse and I'm ready to head out east again or maybe up to Denver for a few days. I came out of it ahead anyway, so my bank account looks better than it did. I'm closer to it even if I'm not quite there yet."

Curtis grinned and slapped his leg a hard whack. "I knew it. I knew you wouldn't stay on even after the rumors said you were the new foreman."

"It was offered," I admitted.

He waved that aside. "Of course it was. That was the least she could do. But I'm not at all surprised. No indeed."

Curtis reached inside his coat and pulled out a folded sheaf of papers. He flopped them on the table between us.

"That isn't a contract," he said, "and it isn't to be signed. I don't think it needs to be. What that is, Cowboy, is an idea. Read it and tell me what you think."

I did and when I was done I looked up again. Probably my eyes were bulging.

"I told you once before," Curtis said before I could speak, "that I have a fondness for the beef industry. Beef is where I got my start, and one way and another it's still the foundation of my affairs. That's why I came here to start with.

"The Triple-X could have been a fine location at the right price. Excellent grass and a rail siding right on the property. That is worth a great deal by itself." He shrugged. "On the other hand, there is a lot of property for sale.

"For instance," his eyes got something of a sparkle into them, "do you know the Trinidad area?"

I nodded. I hadn't worked right in that country, but I had passed back and forth through it by train and by horseback.

"I know of a pretty nice piece northeast of Trinidad. The grass isn't as good as it is here, of course. About fifty or fifty-five acres to the cow unit. No improvements on the land, but a man could go it the old-timey way and put a soddy together in no time at all, make something permanent later on. It works out cheaper than the Triple-X would have on a per cow unit basis, but it would be a three-day drive for shipping and the roads lack bridges. It can be bought at sixty cents an acre. Somewhat higher on terms."

"Oh, Lordy. How much land?"

He told me.

"I could swing that, Curtis."

"Well?" He grinned and shoved his hand across the table for the shake that could change my whole life.

What he was suggesting in that paper that he had prepared before I ever walked in the door was a partnership agreement. Not some hired-man situation but a full damned partnership in a beef-raising venture.

I was to supply the graze and the on-site management. He was to supply the stock cows and the marketing, guaranteeing to buy the beeves at his packing house at a favorable market rate. I knew that with the right accountant and tax man it could be a whale of an investment for him. And for me too.

The deal was that once the herd was started we would go shares on the increase including the she-stuff, which would mean L14 that in a few years I would have a heifer herd building too.

It was a fine deal for the both of us and it damn sure wasn't charity. Curtis stood to make a bundle off his money if I did my part of it the way I knew I could.

"I can't think of anybody I'd rather work with in this, Cowboy," he said, still grinning.

I reached across the table and shook my friend's hand.